Susanna Mitchell was ~~~~~~~~~~~~~~~~~~~~~~~~ ere
she lived until recentl~~~~~~~~~~~~~~~~~~~~~~~ in
London and also with a ~~~~~~~~~~~~~~~~~~~~ She
has had a number of short stories and poems published.

Ms Mitchell now lives in Hampshire with her husband
and two children.

SUSANNA MITCHELL

# The Token

Futura

*For my Mother*

A **Futura** Book

First published in Great Britain in 1984
by John Murray (Publishers) Ltd

This edition published in 1985
by Futura Publications, a Division of
Macdonald & Co (Publishers) Ltd
London & Sydney

*All characters in this publication are fictitious
and any resemblance to real persons, living or dead,
is purely coincidental.*

ISBN 0 7088 2783 7

Printed and bound in Great Britain by
Collins, Glasgow

Futura Publications
A Division of
Macdonald & Co (Publishers) Ltd
Maxwell House
74 Worship Street
London EC2A 2EN

A BPCC plc Company

# 1

Stella sat in the big waiting room and stared at the book on her lap. She had brought a book with her each fortnight, ever since the hospital visits began. This afternoon she had chosen it carefully, filled with fresh resolve that she would not let her concentration fail her; but already she could tell it was useless. The fear was as numbing as ever. The words had begun to swim about as they always did, blurred and meaningless on the open page. Besides, it was so hot in here; she felt she was sitting in an oven. How could anyone read with such heat pressing on their temples? Even her eyes were scratchy and dry.

Perhaps it would be better to abandon the book altogether, to fix her mind on the moment when all this would be over . . . the moment, not long away now, when she would feel the chill and see the dusk of an ordinary January evening; when she would hail a taxi and drive home through the rush hour; when she would make herself a pot of tea.

She shifted miserably. It was absurd how nebulous such pictures became in this stuffy tomb of a building. If only there were some windows. Without windows you became disorientated; you lost all touch with reality. It could be day or night, summer or winter for that matter. It was as if all time had been suspended, petrified for ever under the interminable fluorescent light.

She swallowed, claustrophobia stirred uneasily inside her like a sleeping thing disturbed. It must be defeated, by whatever means lay to hand. It was only a matter of concentration, how often, in the past, had she said that to Mary? Although now, with this new unwelcome insight, she sometimes wished that she had used more compassionate a tone. Mary gasping for air in the lift . . . white-faced and sick on the tube . . . treats ended in frenzied flights from the cinema; it had all seemed tiresome and self-destructive, distastefully uncontrolled. She had been so sure that firmness, rather than pity, was called for. It was foolish to reassess such an old decision, and one which had worked so well.

She shut the book with a snap and stared fixedly at the carpet. It was very ugly, so ugly that once she had thought it almost vicious, but lately she had discovered a fascination in the monstrous design of the thing. You became mesmerised if you stared into its depths for long enough; it absorbed you completely. You could lose yourself in the maze of mustard squiggles, plunge down its riot of turquoise whorls. You shrank to Lilliputian size, ploughing through the hideous nylon pile like an explorer through tropical vegetation, and the feet of the nurses, when they occasionally crossed your vision, loomed enormous. Their thickly stockinged legs rose like trees in a rain forest, and then passed out of sight as you canoed down another electric-blue rapid into the golden whirlpool beneath.

"Mrs. Leonard, please?"

The trees were not moving this time. Intrusively, disappointingly, they were legs again, and the voice that came from somewhere above them already held a note of patient reproach. It was an inflection that Stella particularly detested. She felt she was being reproved as if she was an imbecile, or a very small child.

Slowly, begrudging her obedience, she lifted her head.

The nurse was young. Her face shone with health, pink and white like a new doll. It made Stella feel defeated just to look at her. It was ludicrous, it was humiliating to find herself in the power of this pert little creature, yet before her she withered. She had no weapons to compare with the girl's quelling detachment. In vain she reminded herself that she was admired and respected; that, in these last few years, she had even begun to recognise herself as famous. Stella Leonard. The celebrated sculptress. Articles in the press, interviews on television, collectors squabbling to acquire old carvings. She had shrugged off these honours as matters of no importance, yet surely they should have supported her now, have confirmed her existence? But it had all become irrelevant. Faced with this nurse, Stella

Leonard was no longer a person. Her life, her work, her character, had simply been obliterated. She had become A Patient, a name on a list. It was impossible to retain a scrap of her identity before the complete indifference in that bright impersonal gaze.

She turned her head away. Henry, she thought. Henry.

She conjured him up expertly, relieved that his face came so clearly on demand, bringing comfort and strength when she needed them most. The summoned Henry never let her down, he was always powerful and consoling. Only in dreams was he ever the final Henry; then sometimes she found him haggard, wasting away, with his fine head grown too big for him, the skin stretched taut over his skull. But you never gave in, she thought, remembering his dogged struggle against a heart that refused to support him. I have never had your brand of courage, nor your capacity for hope. I'm frightened, Henry. Help me to find some dignity.

She pulled herself up with a start. The brown pebble eyes were waiting. A small cloud of impatience was creeping into them.

"I'm coming now, Nurse."

Her time-table will run to schedule, thought Stella. I have behaved in the proper manner. Perversely, she suddenly wished that she hadn't. I could have gone into a coma, she thought regretfully, or fallen moaning on the carpet. A nasty scene in the waiting room. Dr. Zuckerman impatient and querulous – 'Where is Mrs. Leonard, Nurse? I thought I asked you to have her waiting?' He would have been disappointed, afraid that his drugs would be wasted. Yes, at least she could have caused the nurse a passing inconvenience.

She rose to her feet, smiling at her own childishness, a little cheered despite herself that she still retained the power of this small choice. But her comfort ebbed as she followed the starched back down the corridor. The friendly carpet gave way to linoleum here, and her feet echoed upon it hollowly, startlingly loud above the pad of the girl's thick crêpe soles.

She felt as though she were being frog-marched to a cell for interrogation, and she looked wildly for something to divert her. The walls were bare and forbidding, a depressing expanse of spotless margarine; but there, proudly displayed on a little table, was a sight that caught her attention, a brand-new extravaganza of plastic flowers. It was engrossingly hideous, a bouquet, a sheaf, a veritable mountain of the things. She studied them avidly, captivated by their ugliness. Who put them there? Who took the trouble to design and renew them? They were clearly meant to be beautiful, to give the patients pleasure. Was she irritated or touched that they should be so grotesque?

She tore herself away, this was certainly no time to loiter. The nurse had stopped a little way ahead of her and was glancing back over her shoulder, tapping her foot on the floor. Contrite, Stella hurried after her and caught her up where the two long corridors intersected.

The consulting rooms lay straight ahead; there she would find outside walls, windows, daylight, but she forced herself to look to the left, back into the maw of the building, where the red lights of the radio-therapy wing winked cheerfully along the walls like a row of fairy lanterns. She knew that one glance would be enough to remind her of what she was escaping, to recreate the inferno of those empty rooms. It proved conclusively that things could be worse, that they had been worse at the beginning. She had no need to turn her eyes to the beds and wheelchairs clinking together in the queue for treatment. The very look of that passage was sufficient to make her almost welcome the thought of Dr. Zuckerman. Anything was better than lying there alone with those huge faceless machines.

Yes, viewed like that there was no doubt that things were improving. This afternoon she had noticed, had found amusing, the odious arrangement of plastic flowers. That alone was an advance. In the early days she had not even seen them. She had been absorbed in her fruitless fight against reality. Her shock, her rejection of the whole idea that she should have cancer, had made the hospital more horrible, the treatment more obscene. She had resented the tests, for fear of what they would uncover; she had not allowed herself to believe the results, or in the merits of the lethal medicines prescribed and

8

her doubt had increased her terror. At least all that was in the past.

Of course, the drugs were still nauseous. It is not easy to swallow pills that kill your body tissue. Nor did she need Dr. Zuckerman to remind her that it was not only diseased tissue they killed. The drugs themselves told her that – the fever they brought; the weakness; the exhaustion. She had seen at once that if she gave them a chance they would kill her cleanly and efficiently, with more authority than the disease that crept like a lichen through her body. They would thwart it by the suddenness of their attack. If she did not want to die by inches, Dr. Zuckerman must continue his treatment. Those bottles of pills, repulsive though they were, had become her salvation, her only allies. She must have them beside her. In the loneliness of her illness they had acquired a personality of their own.

Loneliness. The thought of loneliness was in itself disquieting. She should not be lonely. She would not be lonely if she could bring herself to confess, to confide in Mary. But the thought appalled her. It was more difficult than ever these days to break through the barrier between them; to put things in the proper way. She had so little strength, and her weakness seemed to widen the gulf, to make her more inept at handling their precarious relationship; yet this news must be broken tactfully, tenderly. The right words must be found; there must be no friction between them this time, no misunderstanding. If Mary failed to respond she must not withdraw, she must offer her affection freely, unrequited. . . But she had failed so often. She could hardly expect to break such a painful pattern now.

She sighed, pulling the curtains of the cubicle shut behind her and struggling out of her clothes. It was unbelievable, after all these years, not to know what Mary would feel – how she would react to the news that she had cancer. How much would she mind? Would she be shocked, saddened, deeply affected? But she could not tell. She had never known, really, whether Mary cared for her or not. Lately she had begun to wonder if she positively disliked her? But then she had always wondered that, right from the beginning. Such a remote, difficult child, uncertain of herself, shy and awkward. At first she had tried enthusiastically to win her over, touched by her resemblance to Henry, and by her obvious devotion to him; but even then she had found her unapproachable, proud and prickly, impossible to reassure. Still, she had gone on hoping that Mary would come to accept her; that Robert's arrival would thaw the ice, would make them, all four, into a family.

And it had, of course, in a way. They had been intimate and involved; their lives had interlocked with one another. She did not see Mary as a step-child. Mary was her daughter – just as Henry was her husband, or Robert her son. Sometimes they had been close. Surely they had? Surely Mary had felt it? She could not think why the unease and resentment smouldered on between them; why Mary seemed to look on her as an adversary. She had tried so often to win her confidence and trust.

"Oh, not too bad, thank you, Doctor."

Perhaps she had not tried hard enough. Perhaps she had given up too easily. Those busy crowded years, demanding and exciting. There had been so little time to spare; so little time to get to grips with Mary. They had rubbed along – and anyway, she had had her father; had been marvellous with Robert. In all the hurly-burly it had not been hard to ignore her reticence, to overlook their failure to communicate. It had not seemed such a serious matter. But it was, she thought wretchedly, watching Dr. Zuckerman advance upon her as though she was a slide of cultured cells in a laboratory. It was serious. It is serious. I will soon be leaving Mary, and I don't know what to say.

The doctor's hands were smooth, inanimate and pliable as if they were made of rubber. She shut her eyes so that she would not have to watch them as they prodded and kneaded, exploring her decay. She was glad that it seemed impossible they should belong to a human being; it was best to imagine them as surgical instruments worked by remote control. She could simply strive to detach herself from this degrading moment; from her nakedness; from her ruined body; from the clockwork doctor with the rubber hands.

Henry would rescue her; he would find a way to restore her self-respect. Even though he saw her fear, even though he shared her torment, he would be able to lift her above it, to salvage what was left of her pride. With Henry here she would feel, she would know, that some part of her remained unblemished. He would help her to find and hold on to the knowledge that something within her was unspoilt, was clean and healthy and free.

Behind her shut lids, the picture of him was forming, and she frowned with concentration. But the result was disappointing. She was not at peace with Henry; the comfort he brought was clouded. Perhaps he would look like this, puzzled and dismayed, until she had told Mary?

She shook her head angrily. Could he not see the damage she would do to the girl? Mary would feel responsible for her in this crisis. Even if she did not love her, she would care for her through a sense of duty. She would be a drain on Mary's energy, on her time, on her life. It was useless to pretend otherwise.

But Henry would not have seen it like that. Henry had been blind to any flaw in their relationship – perhaps he had not wanted to find one. 'The child adores you, Stella. Surely you can see that?' And she hadn't argued; she had let him have it that way, since he so plainly desired to believe it. After all, he had enough to bear with Robert.

No, Henry would not understand this deception; and of course, he was right. It was terrible to keep so much from Mary. The lies were becoming so involved, and much less plausible.

She will find out, thought Stella in sudden panic. She will find out quite soon, and then she will not forgive me. I must tell her before she finds out.

Afraid that she had spoken aloud, she glanced covertly at Dr. Zuckerman. But he seemed oblivious to her. He sat at his desk now, like a judge waiting for the court to reassemble. The trial was over, but the sentence was still to be passed.

She tried to read his face, hoping for some clue as to how his mind was working, but she could not see him clearly. The winter sunlight blazed through the window straight in her eyes, and against the glare he loomed blackly, a faceless silhouette. It seemed an eternity before he spoke.

"Your blood is a little disappointing, Mrs. Leonard," he said at last. He sounded reproachful, as if she had lowered her blood count on purpose to obstruct his efforts.

"Though I'm very pleased with our progress," he went on. "Very. The tumour is responding most favourably at present." He paused and repeated almost wistfully, "Yes, really a most favourable response."

Stella waited, and he sighed, wresting himself from the thought of the obedient tumour to the less satisfactory patient.

"Unfortunately," he repeated grudgingly, "I am becoming increasingly anxious about the general state of your health. Especially, as I say, in view of your present blood count."

He feels he cannot go on with the treatment, thought Stella. He has realised he is killing me.

The sun had gone, swallowed abruptly by the bulk of the residential block across the courtyard. The silhouette was a face again, three-dimensional, with the features back in position.

She stared at it bleakly. It wasn't a bad face really, nor a young one, but it was curiously bland and untroubled. It looked as though it had been freshly laundered, every crease meticulously smoothed out. There were no lines, nor wrinkles; no imprint left behind of either joy or suffering. It was difficult to believe that anybody who owned that face had experienced emotion at all. She shook her head; even in her anxiety her professional eye was offended by such dullness. It was shocking for a face to be so barren, so immature; as a model it would be wholly without value.

Still, she had to admit that in a way the thought pleased her. It seemed to reassert her personality, to right the balance between them. How could she fear a face that she had just discarded as a carving?

"I feel surprisingly well, you know, Doctor," she said steadily.

He looked up, pleased. "You do? Well, that is certainly encouraging."

He's proud of his mixture, she thought. These drugs are his life's work, his children. He's longing to give them a chance.

"You don't feel increasingly tired, Mrs. Leonard? No faintness? No breathlessness?"

"Oh, no!" she said eagerly. "I'm fine really. Marvellous."

Was he looking a little astonished? He's no fool, thought Stella. I'm laying it on too thick. "At least, considering everything," she concluded lamely.

But already he was writing on the prescription pad before him.

I've done it, she thought. He can't resist the challenge.

"I feel I should warn you," he said slowly, still scribbling on the paper before him, "that we are nearing the limit of this treatment. These drugs, they can only be used for a restricted time, in a restricted quantity. They are very effective in combating cancerous cells, you see, but regrettably normal cells are also destroyed."

He paused and looked at Stella, as if seeing her for the first time. "Are you sure you understand, Mrs. Leonard? Your body can only tolerate a certain amount of this treatment. After that it becomes – well, dangerous – to continue. A balance must be struck between fighting the disease and keeping you, er . . ."

"Keeping me alive," said Stella, more loudly than she had meant to. "Yes. Of course I know that, Dr. Zuckerman."

Suddenly she was utterly exhausted. She could feel her control slipping, hysteria building up like a boil in the constriction of her chest.

If I stay here much longer, she thought, I will tell this suave young man how little I desire to be kept alive by him and then he will withhold his medicine. He will leave me to die slowly, alone with the cancer, and Mary will have to watch me die.

But he was rising dismissively. "We will try the pills for another fortnight, Mrs. Leonard, as you still feel so well on the dosage. Then another blood test. Should this show further deterioration I shall have to rest you for a little."

He smiled expansively, forgiving her blood for its misdemeanours.

"And now, if you will just go along with Nurse, she will give you your injection."

She had won. It was not a final victory, but it was something.

As she offered her arm to the shining point of the needle, she felt her strength returning. She always welcomed this injection; it marked the final stage of the ordeal. Once it was over, once the syringe was empty, she would put the thought of its contents from her. She would be free to go away.

I will feel better when I have told Mary, she thought. It's always better when you have faced things, isn't it Henry?

And she would face Mary – of course she would. But not this evening. Even Henry would not expect her to tackle Mary tonight, after this horrible consultation.

In a day or two she would be less exhausted. In a day or two she would have stored up her energy; she would be ready for anything. Until then, the thought could be put away. Tomorrow, or the next day, she was bound to feel better.

It was foolish to worry about Mary now, this evening, when soon, despite the drugs and the sickness, she would surely not feel so terribly tired?

# 2

Mary Leonard crossed the reception area with her arms full of files from the meeting and fled through the crowded corridor to her own office. She kicked the door shut and leant against it for a moment as if to barricade herself in.

She had not shone at the conference. And now that she had at last been given a really important account to handle, it was certainly expected that she should shine. It was vital that she should impress them as worthy of her promotion. She should have been brim-full of ideas, a new broom sweeping out old dust with vigour.

What had happened to her flair, her much praised streak for the adventurous? Where had her attention been, when it should have been riveted on the task before her? On Stella, she thought furiously. On Stella and her accursed pills. Bottles and bottles of pills, all labelled with names that meant nothing to her. And a chart, if you please, neatly marked in Stella's own exquisite writing! She must be taking hundreds of the things. What did they mean? Why did she need them? And why, above all, should she find them this morning, the very morning that she ought to have been at her best?

Anger choked her; it was so unfair. It was typical, absolutely typical of Stella to have done this to her. And on top of it all she felt guilty, as if she had been spying. The fact that she had only gone to Stella's bathroom to borrow some toothpaste did not make it any better; she had nonetheless found out something private, something personal and secret, that Stella did not want her to know.

I will have to ask her, she thought apprehensively. Now that I've seen them I've simply got to find out. But how would she begin? How would she explain such a blunder? She could see Stella's face, cold with incredulity, as she listened to the fumbling story of how she had opened a private cabinet in a bathroom that was not hers and found something she was not meant to see. Perhaps she could have redeemed herself if she had instantly shut the door upon her indiscretion, but she had been gross enough to read the labels on the bottles, even to investigate the chart. In Stella's eyes she knew this would be as bad as reading another person's letters; you did not poke and pry in bathroom cupboards that were not your own, any more than you rifled someone else's desk.

Stella frequently closed a subject by refusing to discuss it. She would certainly do so this time, faced with such wanton intrusion. And where will I be then, thought Mary a little wildly. Stella's health will have become another matter we can never discuss together. She won't want to be reminded that I have done such a tasteless thing.

But what was Stella doing with all that medicine? She was not a hypochondriac. She was not a health crank. Stella must be really ill to be harbouring all those bottles. Why could she not have talked to her about it, like any normal person? And why, if she was going to make this horrible discovery, should it have to happen today? So much had depended upon this morning, and now she had thrown it away. She had made a thoroughly bad impression.

This account was a real chance for her, she knew that; and she had worked long enough in advertising to know that if she muffed it, it would not come again. Until now the accounts that she had handled had been run-of-the-mill undemanding affairs that had jogged along of their own volition. But this one was different; there was real opportunity here. Big money was involved too, and a great deal of prestige value if things went well. She had hardly believed her ears when they told her she was to handle it, it was so exactly what she wanted – an old product, of good quality, but out of the limelight with its sales slumping away. She would provide something that would jerk it into present-day consciousness, bring it back with a bang, make it a household word. What a challenge!

If she succeeded, surely even Stella would see what a contribution she had made? But that was asking too much; Stella would never see. Stella did not know the first thing about advertising. She seemed pleased enough that Mary was interested in what she was doing, but she made no effort to understand it, no pretence of thinking it worthwhile.

A couple of weeks ago, on the day she had been given the account, she had come home later than usual after a celebratory drink with Barrie. She had tried to tell Stella then how thrilled she felt; what a great chance this was to prove herself at last. After all, she had worked for Markhams for years now, ever since leaving university. She was nearly thirty. She had waited a long time for this moment to come.

"It's a fine old company," she had shouted above the hammering, stamping her cold feet in the powder that covered the studio floor. "You can bring so much more sincerity into pushing a product you believe in."

Stella put down her chisel and actually looked at her, peering through the dust that swirled round the evolving statue. Mary glanced at it absent-mindedly. It seemed to be a bird. It flashed through her mind then that Stella was not making much progress with this carving. She seemed to be slowing up these days.

"Well," Stella had said dryly, "I don't know about sincerity, but you certainly seem enthusiastic. Keep that up and you will have the whole country duped into buying Barratts' products." She picked up her chisel again and chipped meditatively at an eyelid. "I'm glad to hear they are good," she added, "though if they are, you would think they would sell without your efforts, wouldn't you? On their merits, I mean."

She always says this, thought Mary. She thinks what I do is pointless. An enormous con trick. I might have known 'sincerity' would rile her.

"Oh, products don't sell like that nowadays, Stella," she said for the hundredth time. "They've got to be brought before the public. Properly presented. It's all very competitive."

She glanced up aggressively. 'Competitive' was another word that Stella disapproved of. No one in Stella's world had ever had to be competitive. They were all too talented. Gifted even, thought Mary grudgingly, looking at the eagle.

Stella with her sculpture, famous without wanting it; Father with his tedious books which nobody read but which were so highly respected; even Robert, who made so little effort to excel in anything – even Robert had been described as brilliant at college. And look at the awful rubbish he produced. No, none of them had needed to be competitive. They had had it on a plate, a sense of purpose, a means of fulfilment. Only Mary needed to be competitive.

But Stella had not picked on the word that time. Indeed she did not seem to have heard her. She sat down heavily on an orange-box under the hunched wings of her emergent bird. In the grey light, streaked with the grey dust, her face looked worn and haggard, and Mary had felt the first stirrings of a new anxiety. What was wrong with Stella these days? She'd seemed all right at breakfast.

She crossed the studio and stood behind her, putting her hand with trepidation on the thin powdery shoulder.

"Come and have a drink," she said nervously. "You're looking a bit peaky. You're working far too late."

The hand was thrown off with energy, as she had known it would be. As it always had been.

"Oh, don't worry about me," Stella said briskly. "I work when I feel like it, late or not."

She did not ask Mary's opinion of the eagle.

Why, it's Father! she thought. She felt jolted, shocked. It must be Father. Those were his hooded eyes, that was the set of his head. And the shoulders, or wings rather, were hunched up just as his had been from all the endless poring over his books. Yes, surely it was Father?

Yet how could she say such a thing? 'Stella, is this meant to be Father?'

No. No good. If it was Father then to say so became banal, fatuous, a thing too obvious to be remarked upon.

If it was not? Then what a terrible thing to say! Stella would be outraged, disgusted. She might even be bitterly hurt. No, it could not be risked. Specially not with Stella looking so tired tonight.

"I can't think why you don't make this room more comfortable!" she burst out to hide her confusion. "You spend enough time in it. It's like a tomb." She spoke more rudely than she had intended, still shaken by the sudden sight of Father in that eagle thing, if that's what it was. "Why don't you get some heat in here anyway? You're frozen. Look at you, you're actually shivering!"

She had paused expecting, almost hoping, for the sharp answer that should have come, but Stella only said wearily, "Perhaps you are right, Mary." Her tone, and the dull way she dropped the heavy chisel, made her seem momentarily old, even defeated. Though you did not defeat Stella as easily as that.

She saw, looking back, that in that instant she had realised that all was not well with Stella.

How could she have waited till the morning of her first important meeting to face what she had suspected for weeks?

"What's the matter with you?" she said aloud. "Can't you see you're ruining everything I've worked for?" Her back was still to the door and she pressed the bulky files to her chest like a breastplate. But the resentment refused to oust the worry, and the worry did not have its roots in her poor performance at the meeting.

Her arms were aching. She dumped the files on the desk with a clatter. I must talk to someone, she thought. I'm probably getting the whole thing out of perspective.

The thought was attractive; it made everything look less alarming. Maybe there would not be anything much wrong after all, and she would not have to mention the incident of the medicine cupboard? Perhaps the panic she had felt this morning was based on a false assumption? She was apt to get such things out of proportion now that Father was no longer there.

She looked down at the telephone. She would ring someone now, before her resolve wavered. All right, she felt guilty about that too, Stella would see it as yet another odious betrayal, but even Stella could not force her to keep this anguish to herself.

She wondered if she should ring Barrie. It was comforting just to think of him. Perhaps he would be free for lunch and she could tell him about the conference and what a disaster it had been for her. He would be warm and sympathetic.

She put out her hand to pick up the receiver and saw to her astonishment that it was trembling. No, it wouldn't do. Not Barrie. Not when she was in a state like this. She would distress him. She would make a boring embarrassing companion for him, and he would expect to be entertained and amused.

She handled Barrie very carefully these days, feeling the time had come when he must slip through her fingers. It hadn't been like that at first, when they had been new to one another as lovers, new, and therefore exciting. But now she wasn't so new any more and she wondered how long it would be before he began to find her company tedious. It was not his fault that he had come to mean such a lot to her; that was her foolishness, not his. After all, she had always known that she could not expect her relationship with Barrie to be permanent. Even her introduction had been a warning, though at the time she had not bothered to look at it in that way.

She remembered very well that first casual encounter. It had been one of those parties of Daphne Creighton's; she had only been there for want of a convincing excuse. Daphne was kind and vivacious, with an easy vulnerable charm that made you feel churlish when you turned down her often unwelcome invitations; she proffered them as if she was so certain of giving pleasure. "Like a child who hands you a bunch of weeds," as she had once said to Robert; but Robert, who certainly knew her better, had not agreed. "She just wants to own people," he had said. "It's her way of running your life for you."

Daphne had sat for Robert, and she often wondered what had gone wrong between them. He had painted her boldly: a bizarre, striking portrait that had started well and had ended up as a most disturbing likeness. There was no doubt that it caught Daphne perfectly, but at the same time it contrived to diminish and revile her; it made gross and absurd a lot of little traits that you might otherwise have regarded as charming; it underlined every character defect that you had formerly overlooked; it was a cruel, almost a vindictive, painting. She admired Daphne for displaying it with her usual childish zest. Her amused acclaim made Robert's malice look slightly foolish; for once his carefully prepared weapon had misfired.

That night she had borne down on Mary just as she was thinking of leaving, and had taken her firmly by the elbow.

"There's someone I'd like you to meet," she said enthusiastically. "He's a barrister. His name is Barrie Carrington. Fun, but for heaven's sake don't go losing your head over him. . ."

"Why should I?" said Mary, laughing. "And anyway, what's the matter with him? Is he crazy or crooked or something?"

"He just eats women," said Daphne happily, as though she thought it a most satisfactory diet. "He must have been through a dozen of them since his wife left him. . ."

I wonder were you one of them, thought Mary as she squeezed apologetically between a balding film director and a newly appointed judge; it would be just like you to hand him on so cheerfully. Daphne was always giving you things she had discarded and you did not really want; books that she had half read and could not be bothered to finish; expensive scarcely worn clothes. Well, I don't want your cast-off Don Juans either, she thought mutinously as she finally reached the large loosely built figure in the corner. You choose your own lovers, and I'll choose mine.

She had been wrong though; for once, it had turned out that Daphne's offering suited her to perfection. They were still together too, though she noticed that that seemed to afford Daphne rather less satisfaction.

It had been months before Barrie began to speak about his marriage, and by then she found herself shying away from the subject. She might once have been curious, but by the time he began to tell her, she no longer wanted to hear about his wife; it alarmed her to see how bitter he remained and how little faith he now had in anyone's affection; it hurt her to hear how much he had cared. It was three years now since they had last attempted to live together, but he seemed reluctant to do anything concrete about their separation. "When she asks for a divorce, she can have one," he had said dismissively. "But as far as I'm concerned it's hardly worth the trouble. It's not as though I intend to marry again."

21

Mary had taken the point with as much courage as she still could muster. She supposed she should be glad that he liked her enough to want to make the situation plain. At least she knew now that what he had given his wife was a once-only involvement; he felt he had put all his love and hope into a relationship and it had failed. Why should he repeat a commitment that had caused him so much pain?

"But I'm not a celibate," he had said frankly. "I need sex and I like the companionship of women. Just don't expect too much from me Mary. I'm not much use at giving, nowadays."

So there it was; if desire alone kept him near her, then desire must be kept alive. She must not smother it with demands for anything deeper, nor alarm and bore him with her concern. She must be casual and carefree, as she had been in the beginning; she must not ask too much of him, however generous he seemed to be.

It had been so simple at first, when she was still taking the relationship as lightly as he did; but now it was different. She could no longer pretend to herself that she was not acting a part, and it is not easy to deceive your lover when you see him nearly every day. The strain was beginning to tell. She found herself almost wanting Barrie to end the affair before it became impossible to imagine life without him; she was on edge for signs that his interest was waning. Was he getting irritable? Was he less considerate than he had been? Did he make excuses about meeting her? She would not miss the clues; she had seen them all before. And if that sort of thing begins, I'll get out, she told herself decisively. I won't let it run down into rows and recriminations. It has been too good for that.

It was true that so far she could not possibly fault him. He seemed distressed if he thought she was unhappy. He was concerned and attentive if she was ill. A few months ago, when she had 'flu, he had even managed to impress himself upon Stella, who had grown quite impatient at the frequency of his telephone calls and the need to find vases for his flowers. But she had liked him too; Mary knew that by the length of their conversations. Stella would simply have vanished if she had not thought Barrie appealing; she did not waste her words on people she found to be bores. Listening to the rise and fall of their voices through her bedroom floor, Mary had wondered anxiously whether Barrie would have stayed so long if he had not also enjoyed talking to Stella? But you could not tell; he always had excellent manners. And now she was well again, she must not be tempted to impose on them further.

No, she could not ring Barrie. It would be stultifying for him to have to listen to the story of this morning. Office problems and sick relations – how could she expect him to sit through such a thing? Later she would dress up the story of the meeting until it was more acceptable; she would try to make it funny. It would help to tell someone, even if she had to make light of it. But she knew that however hard she tried, it would be impossible to make light of Stella. She would put the thought of Barrie away.

It will have to be Robert, she concluded without enthusiasm. There was really no one else she knew well enough. She certainly could not discuss Stella's private affairs with a mere acquaintance.

She looked at her watch. He would probably still be in bed, and with Leonie most likely, since neither of them seemed to do any work. She did not know how they managed for money, though it always surprised her how often he sold his paintings. She shrugged. He would just have to wake up for once.

The phone rang longer than she expected and she gritted her teeth when she heard Leonie's slow voice answer.

"I want Robert, please," she said without preamble. "I won't keep him long, but I am in rather a hurry."

Perhaps that would wake Leonie up a bit. Sometimes she took hours to prise Robert away from a painting. Suddenly it had become terribly important to hear his voice, so like Father's on the telephone. She would have liked to stick a pin into Leonie.

"I'm afraid Robert's out, Mary," Leonie was saying. She sounded defensive, sullen. "He won't be back till the evening. Can I give him a message or anything?"

What a maddening voice she has, thought Mary. She felt ridiculously frustrated.

"I want to see him, Leonie," she said crossly. "Could I come round this evening after work? I won't stay long, but there's something I have to discuss with him." She paused but Leonie said nothing. "It's a family matter," she persisted, "I really must see him urgently."

Perhaps 'family matter' would quell her, since she and Robert were not married. And I simply cannot have Leonie in on this one, thought Mary. What would Stella say!

'Well, I suppose so, if it's urgent," Leonie was muttering. She did not sound hospitable. It's not as if I'm always dropping in, thought Mary. I hardly ever go there.

"I'll come around six then," she said briskly. "See you then!" She put down the telephone abruptly.

Really it was absurd to be so disappointed that Robert was not there to speak to her. She hadn't bothered to ring him up for ages. Indeed she had hardly seen him lately, what with working on the new account and spending so much time with Barrie. He would be useless anyway. He always was useless. Look how little help he had been when Father was ill. When Father was dying.

It's you I need, she thought miserably. You would cope with the whole thing in an instant. You never had any problems in getting through to her.

"Father," she said aloud in her empty office. "I need to talk to you, Father."

She pressed her shoulders against the wall to stop them shaking, and covered her face with her hands.

The afternoon was not so bad once she got down to it. There were numerous small routine jobs to be done and the humdrum activity soothed her. The efficiency with which she handled things made up a little for the humiliations of the morning. I'll sort it all out, she told herself. I'll show them next time.

Barrie telephoned during her tea break and suggested meeting for a drink when she left the office. A quick one, he said, he had a brief he must work on later; perhaps they could have a proper evening tomorrow?

Well, why not, she thought. Robert can wait a little. I have spent half my life wondering why Robert is late for appointments. It won't hurt him to do the waiting for a change.

She felt almost cheerful as she struggled into her coat in the cloakroom, and was pleased to find Barrie in the reception area when the lift disgorged her. Dear Barrie. He remained as punctual as ever after all this time.

"Well, how did it go?" he asked at once. She was not expecting that one. She had not thought he would remember about the meeting.

"Awful," she said spontaneously, "I must have been nervous, I suppose. They all seemed to expect so much of me." She put her hand on his arm. "I'm afraid I wouldn't make much of a barrister. Let's go and drown my sorrows."

He looked at her with concern.

"I'm sorry," he said sincerely. "It's not like you to be nervous."

I've let myself down, she thought morosely, refusing to be warmed by the sympathy in his voice.

"Let's go," she said, not wanting him to probe further. "I have had about enough of this place for today."

The January air took her breath away as they turned off the Strand towards the river. It was a dank choking night. Already the lights seemed suspended in grey fuzzy halos, and the rush-hour buses loomed nose to tail, indistinct and enormous, crippled by the thickening fog.

The raw air rasped in their throats and the cold urged them on until she was almost running to keep up with Barrie's long stride, so that they hardly spoke until they reached their pub off the Embankment and swung the doors shut with a comfortable thud behind them.

It was warm inside, dimly lit and crowded. It smelt of beer and damp overcoats. She liked the dark wooden partitions between the tables; you could feel secluded here, despite the press of drinkers. They often chose this pub after work.

She squeezed herself into a stall and sat down gratefully, her icy face already beginning to thaw. She could feel her hair, damp with fog, starting to curl hectically round her head as it always did when she allowed it to dry undisciplined. I may not have inherited Father's intellect, she thought ruefully, but I certainly have his hair. . . Still, Barrie had said he liked it so often that she was actually prepared to believe him.

She looked up at him now as he struggled towards her, holding their drinks high so that they would not be jostled in the crowd. Approaching like that, with his arms held above him, he towered over the crush round the bar. He looked absurdly huge, like the giant in a fairy tale, and the little people around him seemed to melt into the smoky haze. Increasingly she found this failure to focus properly on anyone else when Barrie was there. He was on a different scale somehow. Get him fixed in your eye and everything else faded out.

"Why, hello Gollywog!" he said now as he reached the table. "Nice to see you around again."

She smiled back uncertainly as he wedged himself into the pew beside her. I don't know what to say, she thought. I don't know how to make him laugh this evening. Once I start it will all come out . . . Stella . . . Robert . . . the idiotic way I went to pieces over the presentation. . . Surely I can think of something interesting to tell him? Something amusing. Surely I can make a joke or two?

She stared at his long legs where they stuck out among the feet of the standing customers. She was usually exasperated to see him settle back like this – in a minute or two somebody would trip over him. A stumble; a spilt drink; Barrie surprised and apologetic; it always happened sooner or later if she didn't ask him to move. But this evening it did not seem to matter. This evening the familiar attitude was suddenly precious to her. She felt an irrational longing to keep him like that; to hold and prolong the moment. It was almost as if she would not see him sit in quite that way again.

"Mary!" he said, and she looked up startled, appalled to find how close she had come to tears. Perhaps he hadn't noticed? But his voice was sharp with query – or was it with annoyance? She wondered for the hundredth time how much she gave away when she forgot herself like this and found his eyes upon her, how much he read in her unguarded face?

"I'm sorry . . ." she began, feeling her way, hoping his

expression would guide her. But he interrupted her brusquely, almost rudely.

"Don't be silly," he said. "What do you mean 'you're sorry'? Why should you have to be sorry every time you're worried or sad? Why can't you tell me what's the matter for once, and let us talk it over together? Do you know you still treat me like a stranger, Mary? And a pretty insensitive one at that."

His voice had risen and she stared at him blankly. He sounded really angry, as if she had slighted him in some way. A stranger, he said. Well, had he not asked her, in a fashion, to regard him as a stranger? Had she not tried to do as he wanted, to make him feel free of any commitment? It was his own attitude in this respect that lay at the root of much that distressed her; but she could not say that, of course; and now, in the face of his irritation, all other starting points seemed out of the question too.

"I'm tired," she said stiffly. "I told you I'd had an awful day at the office. And I was going to talk to you about it, if you had given me a little time."

That was true anyway, and saying so made her feel justly aggrieved, less inclined to disgrace herself by crying. It seemed a long time, nonetheless, before he replied.

"All right," he said at last. "All right. I've snapped at you when you're down and I'm really very sorry."

He did not sound sorry. He sounded offended and cold; but he picked up her untouched glass and put it in her hand, closing her fingers round it as if she had been a child, and she knew he wouldn't press her further. She was glad of that, since she found she no longer wanted to talk about the meeting, she would be incapable of embellishment tonight anyway. She just wanted to be peaceful for a little, to sit in the warmth and noise and feel Barrie beside her.

"Barrie," she said, "do you mind, would you understand, if I said that I'd rather not talk about the meeting? Not tonight anyway. I've thought of nothing else all day, and I badly need a break."

She peered anxiously into his face, but it seemed unusually expressionless.

"I thought it might help," he said. "I thought it might help to tell me about it – whatever went wrong this morning. It's good to share things, especially problems, now and again, Mary. But if you don't feel like talking about it this evening, of course I understand."

The tone was light and yet she knew he expected something from her, but really, she couldn't start on the meeting now. If he wanted her to talk sincerely, then it would be impossible to explain the day at all without embarking upon Stella.

"I'll tell you later," she said. "Everything. All about it."

He sighed. "Oh, just as you like. It doesn't matter if it's such an effort for you anyway. For heaven's sake, don't feel that you HAVE to tell me anything."

He's hurt, she thought. I didn't mean to hurt him.

She put down her glass and felt for his hand.

"Look," she said rather desperately, "of course I want to tell you about the meeting, but not just now. I'm tired. I want to forget it. And I've got to go and see Robert in a minute. We haven't got very long to talk about anything this evening."

"Can't I come with you?"

She shook her head. "I wish you could, but it wouldn't do. Really, Barrie. There's a – well, a family problem to sort out between us, and I've got to see him on my own, I'm afraid."

He laughed suddenly. "It's hopeless," he said. "I give in. Seems I'm always superfluous to requirements!"

It was not a happy laugh, and the words, thrown off so casually, carried a sting that dismayed her. She was not used to Barrie in this mood and she looked at him uneasily, wondering how to respond. Perhaps she should refute his remark; but then it had been a joke. It might make things worse to appear to take it seriously.

In any case, before she could speak, his anger seemed to have evaporated. He put his arm round her and began to tell her about the new brief he was handling, pulling her tangled head against the bulk of his shoulder.

I don't know why he puts up with me, she thought. I'm a nervous wreck, and it's showing. But perhaps this once it wouldn't matter, she would try to make up for it another time.

She sat there limply, listening to the cadence of his voice, watching his hand on the table. She began to feel sleepy and relaxed.

I don't want to struggle with Stella, she thought drowsily. I don't want to struggle with Robert either. And I don't want to face up to losing you, and all the emptiness that you'll leave behind you.

She closed her eyes for a moment. I need not think of that now, she told herself consolingly. Tonight I will just accept that you have become an addiction. I'll find the strength to give you up from somewhere, when I have to. But not now. Not tonight.

# 3

Stella knelt in the attic with the suitcases around her. Their
contents brimmed over in riotous disorder onto the uncarpeted
floor, letters, photographs, cuttings from newspapers; book
reviews of Henry's, interviews for magazines. Jumbled and
chaotic, a mountain of souvenirs lay there before her, telegrams, postcards, catalogues from exhibitions; concert pro-
grammes, bank statements, the children's school reports, all
the trivia and all the triumph. And what does it amount to,
thought Stella, except a pile of rubbish that will soon mean
nothing to a living soul?

She looked round her helplessly; the sheer volume of the
stuff was daunting. She felt swamped in paper, harried by
memories. I should throw it all out, she thought. I should burn
the rest of the suitcases unopened. But she knew she could not
do it. It would seem disloyal to turn her back on all these relics
and mementoes. She would feel she was rejecting them, denying the years they brought back so poignantly, negating the
past. No, she was compelled to sift through all this paper; it
would be faithless and ungrateful to dismiss as litter what was,
after all, the record of her life.

She pulled the one empty suitcase towards her. There was
not much worth keeping, but one or two things might perhaps
interest the children – she would pack them into that. Those
newspaper cuttings, for instance? She was sure she had put
them near her; but they seemed to have melted into the grey-
ness of the evening, and she remembered with annoyance that
the light bulb had burnt out weeks ago and she had not
bothered to replace it. Now it was already getting dark, and
from where she crouched by the window she could scarcely
make out the far walls of the attic. The lop-sided tailor's
dummy, the haphazard piles of trunks and boxes, the long-
dead parrot's bird-cage, were blurring and receding in the

fading winter light.

I shall have to fetch a candle, she thought resentfully, glaring round at the gathering twilight; but a candle meant going downstairs to the kitchen, and she knew she would not have the stamina to climb back again. She should have started this job in the morning, she knew that too, but the mornings were so precious now. It was only in the mornings that she still felt strong enough to carve. And you're so nearly finished, she thought urgently. I have got to complete you, Henry. I only hope I'm still able to do you justice.

The thought brought an uneasiness foreign to her nature, and she glanced at her hands, frowning, as if she suspected them of letting her down. Surely the vision was pure, was as vibrant as ever? If she was failing, then it was a failure of execution, born of the weakness, the sickness, the remorseless pressure of working against time. There would be a certain poetic justice in her failure now, when time had run out, when there could be no second attempt at this final, this supremely important carving. It would be a back-payment on all the acclaim, the easy successes. Perhaps she had been too lucky? Perhaps she had grown complacent over the years?

She sighed, sitting back on her heels. Henry had not achieved fame. His public had been small, reserved – a scholarly minority. It made her feel guilty to remember how hard he had worked on his volumes, how he had ground on with painstaking concentration through months, through years of research. In contrast, her own good fortune seemed unmerited.

But I did not strive for recognition, she thought. I enjoyed it, but it was not important. All the joy, all the fulfilment, was in creation – despite the mistakes and the set-backs, and the bad times when I have found myself following the wrong road.

She felt perversely cheered by the memory of all those crises, of the periods of anguished reassessment. Surely no one could call her smug? She had hardly experienced a moment of total satisfaction. There was no reason to believe that the edge of her talent had been blunted by too much achievement, and that now she was being asked to pay the price – though she had to admit that never before in her life had she endured such abject fear of failure.

"What's wrong with my eagle, then?" she said aloud. "What's bothering me about it?"

She shook her head, disheartened by the silence, and gazed abstractedly at the letter in her hands. It was an old letter, the page creased and faded, the writing large and unformed. Mary's.

That was it. Of course. It was because of Mary. She had let Mary's lack of reaction undermine her confidence, unsettle her mind. How foolish she was! By now she should be used to lack of sensitivity in Mary. It was ridiculous to be troubled by it. Yet it had been disturbing to see how completely blind she was to the significance of this carving. If it was any good surely the resemblance would be violently striking? Surely even Mary?

She looked again at the letter in her hands.

"Dear Father," she read. "The exams are nearly over. I hope it will not make you sad to hear that I won't have done very well."

Poor little girl. Poor little Mary. What a bewildering child she had been; so strung up, so uncertain of her ability! Exams, for instance, she had always excelled in examinations. But by the time the results came through the child would have made herself ill with the dread of certain disaster. No amount of experience had ever increased her confidence. I wish I had been more patient, more understanding, she thought sadly, but at the time it was all so irritating and repetitive. I couldn't see why she doubted herself, or why it mattered to her so much.

She tore the letter across and dropped it into the bulging hessian sack beside her. No point in keeping old bundles of notes from the children. They would have no message to offer, once she herself was dead.

A wave of nausea swept over her. She had always been so full of vitality – it was incredible to think that soon she would be dead. Perhaps she should have prepared herself for this illness? But there had been no time for such morbid consideration; she had never thought much about how her life would end. At the back of her mind she had always assumed death would be a

32

sudden affair – a brisk snuffing out that would allow no opportunity for worry, a thunderbolt that would strike her down – but this long-drawn-out process of dying was very different. It was an outrage; an insult. She had always prided herself on the fact that she was tireless, yet here she was already too weak to work for more than an hour at a time.

But I shall finish my bird, she thought, swallowing the terror. For Henry's sake. For the sake of all this – rubbish. She stared round bleakly at the sea of paper. Yes, the carving must be finished. Perhaps it would show the meaning of the confusion round her. It might forge a whole from all these disjointed fragments.

She could see now that it would be far more sensible to conserve her strength for the studio, rather than fritter it away up here. She would just tidy away the worst of the shambles, and then she would forget about the attic until the eagle was finished. In any case it would soon be dark.

She began to gather the letters together and tie them into bundles, but it was surprisingly difficult to resist dipping into them now that she had begun. She picked up a wad of telegrams, and thumbed through them, smiling. They were telegrams of congratulation, mostly on her marriage; on Robert's birth; on the openings of a score of shows and exhibitions. She had forgotten what most of them referred to, and some of them seemed to come from strangers, but she still found herself warmed and gratified by their flattery; it seemed a shame to throw them away. Here was one from someone called Roland. "Completely captivated – congratulations on thrilling exhibition." Which exhibition had that been, and who was Roland? She could not remember. Yet how heartening of him to have cabled her, people had always been so kind.

It was a pity to find that such an encouraging collection was marred by a number of telegrams from Robert, though on reflection it was hardly surprising, Robert had often resorted to telegrams when he feared recrimination on the 'phone. She loosened the clip and pulled them free, glancing at them with distaste. Athens, Paris, Madrid – a tale of accidents, evictions, trouble with the authorities; and all of them asking for money –

"Cable funds by return." She dropped them into the hessian sack with a grimace. There was certainly no pleasure in keeping telegrams from Robert.

She glanced back at the remaining sheets, but they no longer held her attention, and she laid them neatly beside the suitcase. Somehow the thought of Robert had soured the comfort they brought, had robbed them of significance. It was still hard to admit how much Robert's development was disturbing her, for she had always tried to gloss over such anxiety while Henry was alive.

Indeed, it still seemed churlish to doubt her son, or question his personality, for without him there would have been no Henry. She had enjoyed more than twenty years of astonishingly happy marriage, and without Robert they would never have begun.

She smiled suddenly, remembering the shock, and her first horrified reactions. She had never contemplated marriage, her career had absorbed all her energies in those days, and she had worked compulsively, without regard to the feelings and rhythms of ordinary mortals. Henry had been welcome for his devotion. He was a stimulating companion and a foil, when needed, for her moodiness and her emotions. She had not for a moment seen him as a husband; the very thought was intrusive and absurd.

She had shut her mind to the early signs of Robert's arrival, wilfully ignoring the changes in her body. She had always been so careful; she was not an inexperienced girl. You did not conceive accidentally at forty, it simply was not possible. She supposed she must be in for an early menopause.

It was not until months had passed that she finally admitted to herself that she was pregnant, and she had turned to Henry in fury and despair. What could be done? Permanent relationships were stultifying and tedious; she must remain free. This calamity must be averted, he need not think that now he could marry her, trap her.

But she had underestimated Henry. He had been wonderful, wholly compassionate. Without argument he had said that he would arrange for an abortion, if that was what she wished. She must not worry about money, or about his feelings. Above all, she must remain calm, or her work would suffer. Calm. She must remain calm. He would see to it all.

And I became calm, she thought, shamefaced even now at the compliant reaction. I grew calm all right, and fat, and languid. I produced pretty little terracotta heads, and a large tranquil carving 'with a new maturity' the critics said, 'a fresh element that had so far been lacking in my work'. And all the while, Henry was rushing round, gaunt-faced, arranging for my abortion. He did not see that I was quietly giving in to the clamour of my hormones, that I was living from day to day, gestating contentedly, like a cow in a field of spring clover.

It had not been easy to find a doctor willing to undertake such a late termination. By the time Henry gently announced that all was ready, the baby had quickened. She was already a mother, careful, protective, geared to her physical needs; resting, eating, carrying herself as the foetus dictated.

Even then, if Henry had been different, she could still have gathered her tattered dignity together. If he had crowed over what was, after all, his triumph, she might still have asserted her pride over her body. But Henry did not see life in those terms; he did not score up victories. He had simply been enraptured, like a child handed an unexpected gift; had laughed with delight and swept her out to a meal she still remembered, squandering the abortion fee on flowers, on champagne. There could be no going back, his joy was so complete, so touching. And in the event, she had never regretted that extraordinary decision, made for her, against all normal inclination, by her unborn child. Most women felt gratitude to their husbands for giving them their sons. She felt beholden to her son for giving her her husband.

She ran her hands through her hair. It was still amazing, still almost incomprehensible, that Stella Herriot, that unfettered self-centred Stella of forty years' standing, had been transformed so easily into a new personality called Stella Leonard, loving wife, hopeful mother. The old Stella had still been there, certainly; but only as a part of the new, deeper more expansive Stella who had emerged from nowhere and taken over the original model. Even her more acid friends, who had seen the arrangement as a temporary measure only, had admitted that it seemed to be suiting her. It was as if, after an age of icebound repression, she had suddenly burst into flower.

She drew her breath in sharply, as if someone had struck her. She found that grief seized her like this, suddenly and unbearably. After three years it was still as raw as ever.

But the flower did not wither, Henry, she thought. Not while you were with me. We had a good marriage – a passionate marriage – though no one would have thought you a passionate man. You struck my friends as correct and undemonstrative. And the books you wrote, those dry authoritative volumes on Mediaeval Law, they were frigid and formidable too. Only lusty, full-blooded Robert, bouncing round them with animal exuberance, had refuted the picture of two rather chilling studious people, passing coolly into middle age. And so she had been, she still was, inordinately proud of Robert. She was childish enough to care that the world should not mistake her very physical union with Henry for one of dessicated propriety. No one could look at Robert and think that; he had always been vital, handsome, sparkling, the very personification of a love-child.

No, it had not been easy to think unkindly of Robert, who unknowingly had given her so much. Her nature was critical and exacting, but she knew she had been an over-indulgent mother. . .

She picked up an album and leafed through it. There he was, such a beautiful baby; such a lively, charming boy.

Of course she remembered the lies and wildness of his childhood; the violent tantrums, the schools that refused to keep him, how could she forget them? But looking down at the photograph before her, she found it hard, even now, to blame him. He had been gloriously untamed, reckless in his rejection of their values, innocent in his refusal to discipline what talent he possessed.

But there was no doubt that he was a worry: his drinking, his fecklessness, the way he ran through money. It was almost a relief that Henry was no longer here to suffer the anxiety with her, for now she would have been unable to reassure him. In the past it had been different, she had clung tenaciously to her belief in Robert. In her optimism, she had offered comfort to Henry with real sincerity.

"It's just a phase," she had said, how often? "He will grow out of it. It will pass."

Now she was not so sure, and the words would have sounded hollow.

I made myself blind, she thought, staring at the young face that smiled back at her so jauntily. I should have come to terms with this long ago, when you were little. Perhaps I could have changed you. Could I? Could anyone have changed you?

She put her hand to her forehead. She was feverish today. She was always feverish on the days she took the Livamisol; it produced a nightmare sensation of unreality, as if she was wading through some odious green mist. All the drugs seemed to have their own colourful aura, just as all their containers were banded in colourful adhesive tape – bright nursery shades to correspond with Dr. Zuckerman's carefully explicit chart. It struck Stella as obscene to package such lethal doses as if they were sweets for a children's party.

Her throat constricted at the thought of them and she swallowed. She wondered how much longer she would manage to get them down. Perhaps there would not be very much longer. Let there just be time to finish the eagle, she thought desperately, I only need a week or so now. I should not overtire myself like this. I must rest.

She rose stiffly from the floor and leant against the window embrasure. It was sharp and cold and the pressure hurt her. She remembered that she must not lean heavily on sharp edges anymore, everything seemed to bruise her; dark spreading bruises from which her eyes recoiled in disbelief. A vision of the Warfarin bottle, banded with its loathsome scarlet tape, flashed suddenly before her. But Warfarin has a purple aura, she thought in confusion. Purple and black.

She pressed her fingertips against her eyes. Thank goodness Mary had said she would not be in this evening. She could not have coped with Mary now, when she felt so particularly muddled and strange.

"But I will tell her," she said aloud, as if to ward off an accusation. "There's nothing to shrink from."

Of course there was nothing to shrink from. It was not as if Mary would falter. She faced disaster bravely, as Henry had done. She would be competent and practical, she would not try to evade the issue. Perhaps it was the prospect of seeing her death reflected unadorned in Mary's truthful eyes that had appalled her? But surely she had come to terms with death by now?

The stairs were steep, and in the dusk the house below lay cold and unwelcoming. She groped her way to the study and sank into a chair. She felt groggy, airy with tiredness, as if she was drunk. As she turned on the light she glanced up at the desk beside her, seeking, by habit, the comfort of Henry's face. The silver frame winked back at her, but his expression seemed stern and unyielding. Was he looking at her with reproach?

"You know I have never reached her," she told the photograph, bitterly. "You must know how hard I have tried. And it's worse this time, when what has to be said can only bring her sorrow. I won't do it right. . . Oh, why do we always hurt each other, Henry?"

The lamplight shone on the glass, dazzling her with its reflection, obscuring his face. She glared at it, lost and disappointed. Henry did not understand.

"I don't even know if she will miss me," she burst out. "And if I bring her pain, you know she will try to hide it.

"How can I make her see how sad I am to leave her, when she has never understood how dear to me she has become?"

# 4

Mary had always sympathised with Robert's decision to live on the river. The noisy active stretch of water appealed to her. She liked the jumble of houseboats and barges that jostled side by side, and the bright little gardens that sometimes sprang up beside the moorings. She liked the people who lived there too; they were tatty and colourful as their boats, and their oddness and self-sufficiency seemed to have banded them together. She felt they had secured the best of both worlds with their easy camaraderie and their independence. They had managed to remain Londoners and yet had set themselves tranquilly apart.

In the beginning, she had thrown herself with gusto into Robert's plans for the old barge he had bought. It was a ramshackle thing, little more than a hulk when she had first seen it, and black with age and dirt, but she had known at once how delightful it could be. She could picture it in her mind's eye – scrubbed, caulked and painted without; carefully replanned and refurbished below. There would be a lot of hard work, but the results would certainly be worth it; and besides it would do Robert good to put his mind to something practical for a change. How satisfying it would be when at last it floated, solid and restored, beside its neighbours on the river.

It was a charming dream, and in the early days she had pursued it ardently, whether for herself or Robert she hardly knew. At any rate, she had spent a lot of time down at Chiswick helping him to cope with the worst of the problems. Together they had cleared away mounds of rubbish, pumped out filthy water, sealed up the cracks and the drips and the leaks. Toiling side by side, fired momentarily by the same vision, her mistrust had melted as it had not done since they were children. It was good to be working with Robert, she had forgotten that he could be so companionable. Even his friends had responded to the atmosphere of the river, made more congenial by the unusual air of industry and purpose, encouraged by finding Robert at his most appealing.

Now, as she groped through the mist towards the invisible water, Mary found herself flushing at the memory. It was humiliating, after years of increasing resistance, to know that she could still be disarmed by the sunny side of Robert. She remembered with annoyance how childishly eager he had seemed; how open to her suggestions; how appreciative of everyone's efforts. But his enthusiasms had always been frail things, they never survived long periods of hard work. The amount of effort required alone should have told her it was hopeless.

How could I possibly have thought it might last, she thought sourly. When has Robert ever seen anything through to the end? It was unfair to blame Leonie for what was, after all, inevitable. Looking back, she realised that anyway the weekends had begun to lose their magic. The familiar Robert had been creeping back, showing all the well-known signs of disenchantment. He was beginning to be bored and indifferent – irritable and lazy by turns. He had started to drink again. Leonie had merely slammed a door which was inexorably closing.

Mary shivered, standing on the blackened deck, listening uneasily to the muttering of the water. The warmth that Barrie had generated, and which had sustained her so comfortably in the security of the taxi, seemed to have dissolved into the fog around her, into the unseen lapping river. She could feel the barge around her, neglected and dilapidated, the depressing remains of all that wasted zeal, and suddenly she could have cried with vexation and sadness. It was no use denying that she cared for the boat; worse – that it had stirred up the depths of her affection for her brother. How could she have allowed him to dupe her again, when of all people, she should have known better? She felt almost more angry with herself than with Robert.

She could hear somebody coming now, and the footfalls were heavy and lethargic; Leonie's. She calmed herself with an effort. She had hoped to find Leonie had gone to bed early, was cooking, feeding her baby, anything that would keep her out of the way. Robert might be hurtful and disappointing, but at least he was always easy company. He was a good listener, attentive and sympathetic; everyone found it relaxing to talk to Robert. It was astonishing how even the most prudent people made him their confidant. It was not until you had left him that you wondered unhappily had you said too much? Those amusing anecdotes he had produced to cheer you up, for instance; were they not in fact the confidences of others? At least I'm through that stage, thought Mary thankfully, remembering with shame her past indiscretions and the havoc he had wrought with them. He'll have no more fun at my expense.

Leonie was peering round the door as if she expected to find a burglar or a ghost. In the swirling mist beneath the light her face looked paler than ever, and there seemed to be black smudges upon it. Perhaps it was dirty.

"Leonie!" said Mary, trying to infuse some warmth into her voice. "I'm sorry I'm so late. I'm afraid I got delayed by a colleague." She paused hopefully, but there was no response, and she hurried on, indicating the weather as if she had just brought it with her, "The fog is really frightful. It took me ages to get here too."

I don't know why I'm apologising to Leonie, she thought with annoyance, she must be used to waiting by now. Robert would never make such excuses. He just expects you to be delighted when he finally turns up.

As if she had spoken her thought aloud, Leonie opened the door a little wider.

"He's out," she said. "Robert. He hasn't come back."

Mary stared at her in dismay. "I thought you said he would be in about six or so?" she said accusingly.

It was so difficult not to adopt this hectoring tone with Leonie, she seemed to invite it somehow. Though in all conscience, thought Mary, she could hardly be held responsible for Robert's lack of punctuality.

"I told you what *he* told *me*." She didn't sound defensive, just indifferent. "You'd better wait a bit anyway, now you are here," she went on. "I suppose he'll be back some time."

She turned away as if the matter held no further interest, and started slowly down the steep stairs that led from the superstructure on deck into the belly of the barge.

Mary followed her reluctantly. She always shrank from her first sight of the huge room that had promised to be so lovely, and the prospect of sitting there alone with Leonie for goodness knows how long filled her with gloom. Moreover, if Robert stayed out very late, then he was almost certainly drinking, and the thought of her vigil ending with the arrival of a Robert too drunk to be of any help to anyone was not reassuring. Still, she had just spent over an hour in a fog-bound taxi trying to get here, and would probably take as long to get home. She supposed she would have to sit it out and hope for the best. She wished she could be sure that Leonie would not produce any of her revolting coffee.

The great keel beam of the barge, standing almost to knee height, divided the hold from stem to stern. They had planned to build the living quarters around it, making it useful as well as attractive. There were so many things that could be done with it. They had seen it as a shelf in the living room, for magazines and gramophone records, or as an inviting bench scattered with cushions and rugs; when they divided off the kitchen it would separate the working from the dining area, pot plants would look splendid on it. Mary had spent a lot of thought on that beam.

Now, picking her way across it, she reflected wryly that it had certainly turned out useful. There was hardly a square inch of its length that was left empty. It was littered with ashtrays and empty mugs and bottles; paper handkerchiefs, babies' dummies, soiled bibs and saucers full of odds and ends. Where Mary crossed it it bore a dishcloth, a hairbrush and a banana skin. She sighed as she looked up and met for the first time Leonie's watchful gaze. She really looks awful, she thought with sudden anxiety, and what has she done to her arm? She was carrying it awkwardly and it seemed to be heavily bandaged, done up in an ineffectual kind of a sling.

"What's the matter with you?" she said, more gruffly than

42

she had meant to. "Have you broken your arm?"

Leonie flinched, whether at her tone or from pain it was hard to determine.

"I fell," she said simply, as if that closed the subject. Then seeing Mary's expectant face she went on reluctantly. "I was coming down the stairs, yesterday evening. They're very steep, those stairs, and I was carrying the baby." She paused for a moment.

"I couldn't help it," she added defiantly, as though she was being accused of some intolerable clumsiness.

Mary looked at her in horror. What had happened to the baby? She looked about her, searching the room for evidence of his survival.

"Is he all right?" she said. "Your baby, I mean? Is he hurt? Did you drop him?"

She felt a surge of real fear. She liked Leonie's baby. He was such a cheerful, placid creature, with his toothless grin and friendly disposition; nothing seemed to upset him. She often felt he should have a medal for looking so wholesome in the midst of all this squalor. It would be terrible if he were injured.

"He'll be all right," said Leonie quickly. She sounded gentle suddenly, reassuring. "He's rather bruised, that's all. I got the doctor for him and he said he had cracked a couple of ribs. He took us to the hospital. They set my arm and strapped Toby up a bit." She seemed proud of her initiative.

"He's over there," she went on, gesturing towards a cot in the corner. "Why don't you go and talk to him while I make a cup of coffee? He likes you. You always get on well together."

"I'd love to," said Mary warmly. She felt an overwhelming relief. Nothing had happened to Toby. She would bear the coffee stoically as a thank offering.

She bent over the cot and smiled at the baby. He was awake, staring at the ceiling with a hostile look she had never seen before. He certainly looked pretty battered. She opened her bag and scrabbled through it for something to divert him. Her powder compact would do. It was blue enamel with her initials in the corner, and she was particularly fond of it; Barrie had given it to her for Christmas. Still, it was the only shiny thing she could find; she would get it back in a few minutes. She poked it through the bars of the cot and he grasped it eagerly, venturing a doubtful smile. He really was a sweet baby. She wondered what his father had been like, and why Leonie had left him and come to Robert. He must have been kind, she thought, to have produced such an agreeable child. Toby would not be so loving if he had been Robert's baby.

"Poor little thing," she said softly, looking at the bruises. "You'll be better soon."

She put out a hand to stroke his head and was shocked to see a look of stark terror flash into the upturned face. He screamed hysterically and lifted his arms as if to shield his forehead. Mary snatched away her hand as if he had bitten it and stared at him in astonishment and distress. What had she done? She had not even touched him. Anyway she was sure it was fear, rather than pain, that had caused him to flinch like that and try to cover his face. She had never known him afraid of anybody, certainly not of herself. Leonie had once said that he liked her particularly because she looked so like Robert, and she thought that was probably true. It was not just Henry's hair and eyes that created a resemblance; it was the way they walked, moved, carried themselves. It had always surprised her that, with only one parent in common, they were very unmistakably brother and sister.

Now, looking down at the wary tear-stained face in the cot, she suddenly knew with unpleasant clarity, exactly what the baby had thought. With the dim light behind her he wouldn't have seen her very clearly, just the silhouette of her hair and the way she moved.

"He mistook me for Robert," she said aloud in bewilderment, "and he was frightened. He thought I was going to hit him."

She swung round on her heel and came face to face with Leonie. She was holding out a steaming coffee mug in her one good hand.

"He thought I was Robert," she repeated stupidly. "He wouldn't let me touch him."

She waited for Leonie to offer some explanation, to convince her she was wrong, perhaps. But Leonie simply bit her lip and said nothing. She looked so downtrodden, with her silence and her bruises and her bandages. You would think I was going to hit her too, thought Mary, in sudden fury. What on earth is the matter with the girl?

She reached out and took the coffee before it began to slop over. She's probably still shocked from the fall, she thought more charitably. I am sure she should be in bed.

"Look," she said as gently as she could, "you're obviously exhausted. You should be sleeping, not sitting up talking to me. I'll just drink my coffee and be off. There's not much point in waiting for Robert anyway, he may not be in for ages. Can I ring for a taxi?"

She moved towards the telephone as she spoke and paused in surprise as Leonie snatched at her arm.

"Don't go!" she said shrilly. "Please stay with me Mary. Don't leave me." She paused, making an obvious effort to steady herself. "I'm sorry," she said more calmly. "It's just that I would love you to stay for a little while if you are able. Just till Robert comes back."

She looked so white and wretched, clutching on to her sleeve, that Mary instinctively put her arm around her, but it seemed the wrong thing to do. As if overpowered by the affectionate gesture, Leonie rested her head on the proffered shoulder and burst into tears.

Mary recoiled, and immediately hated herself for her reaction. She knew that one of her worst sins was this automatic withdrawal from the emotions of others. Tears, hysteria, unexpected intimacy did not so much repel her as leave her totally at a loss for a suitable response. Herself reserved and undemonstrative, she felt inadequate to the demands of the unrestrained; she could not meet them with the freedom of expression they found so easy. It was as if they spoke another language to which she had no key; when she tried to use it she became inarticulate, she could not convey her understanding or her sympathy. Or in Stella's case, she thought suddenly, my love. She was surprised at the thought and the vivid way it had presented itself. Love was a word she seldom brought herself to use. Love should be self-evident, not in need of declaration; it would be belittled in some way if it needed to be confirmed in speech. But was it so obvious, she wondered uneasily. Did Stella know she loved her? Surely she knew?

She tore her thoughts away from Stella and looked helplessly at the sobbing girl who still clung to her shoulder. She felt no affection for Leonie, and the closeness of her body was unpleasing, her unrestrained grief almost indecent. But she needed help, that was obvious, and there was no one else to give it. She could not simply pat her shoulder and go home, as she now longed to do.

The light from the unshaded bulb fell directly on Leonie's upturned cheek as she looked at her. It was her uninjured cheek, or so Mary had supposed, seeing it in comparison with the other. Now at close quarters she saw that it was bruised also; a curious pattern of little bruises, four in a row about level with her cheek-bone, one larger round her jaw. As her eyes took in the marks, Mary knew with a sickening jolt what they represented. Four fingers and a palm; the print of a hand. She did not wonder for an instant whose hand they belonged to. Leonie would have told her if some stranger had attacked her; even she would have made no mystery of that. And the baby, hurt and frightened, his easy innocent confidence gone.

"Robert!" she cried in anguish, as if he would suddenly appear to refute this new horrible knowledge. "Robert!"

She swung Leonie out to face her and took her by the shoulders. She felt a wild irrational desire to shake her, as if she was in some way responsible for this terrible thing Robert had done.

"It wasn't an accident, was it?" she said. "Robert's been beating you up, hasn't he?" She was almost shouting with anger and anxiety. "Why didn't you tell me," she went on. "Why do you try to shield him? It was Robert who injured the baby and broke your arm."

Her hands were clenched tightly on the girl's thin shoulders, and Leonie was staring at her with frightened eyes, nodding dumbly. She seemed too scared to speak. My God, thought Mary, what am I doing? I'm as bad as Robert. She dropped her hands.

46

"I'm sorry," she said more quietly. "I'm afraid it's a bit of a shock for me too. Come and sit down and tell me what has happened."

She led Leonie to the sagging sofa and pulled her down beside her, thrusting the still warm cup of coffee into her hand. "Here, drink this," she said. "Or have you any brandy?" Leonie shook her head. "Well, whisky then. Anything. I think we could both do with a bit of Dutch courage."

"I threw it away," said Leonie miserably. "All of it. Overboard. I did it this morning after we came back from the hospital. I thought that if there was nothing to drink at least it might get us through the evening. But he was so angry. Oh Mary, I have never seen him so angry when he was sober. He said if I didn't want him drinking at home then he would go and do it elsewhere. He never even asked for Toby, he must have known he had hurt him. He just rushed out into the dark and he hasn't come back."

Fresh tears came into her eyes and she looked pleadingly at Mary. "I know I said he hadn't come in all day," she went on, "but he was only here for a few minutes. He went for a drink at once and found it was missing. After that I couldn't tell him you were coming. I couldn't tell him anything."

She put her fist to her mouth and bit her knuckles.

"I'm so frightened, Mary. He'll come back drunk again, I know he will. He picks up Toby and when he cries, he's furious. He flings him down just anywhere, as if he was a sack or something. And last night he kicked him." Her eyes dilated with horror at the recollection. "He kicked him into the keel beam – that's what broke his ribs and bruised him so. I thought he was going to kill him. I pulled him off and he hit me; I must have broken my arm as I fell. I remember lying there thinking that he would probably finish us off this time, but he stopped then, I don't know why. I heard him being sick in the bathroom, and I think he went straight out, after that. Anyway, I didn't see him again till this evening." Her voice petered out and she slumped back against the sofa.

Mary sat rigid; her heart seemed to have fallen into her stomach. I shall be sick myself in a moment, she thought, I know I will. She rubbed her sleeve across her eyes as if to erase the picture of Robert brutally kicking the screaming child. I must pull myself together, she thought. I must do something to help them. What was it that Leonie had said that struck her as so particularly ominous? 'I thought he would probably finish us off this time.' This time? Then there must have been others.

"Has this been going on for long?" she asked hoarsely. Her voice sounded dry and cracked, as if she had a sore throat. "Has he hurt you, has he hurt Toby, before last night?"

"Only when he is drunk," said Leonie quickly. "He's only violent when he has been drinking." She sat up straight again and looked at Mary with a kind of weary dignity. "He can be so gentle, you know," she said wonderingly. "He's so generous, so merry. He can be such fun. He makes me feel alive, somehow – as if everything was new and exciting. And he loves Toby really. I . . . I know he does. If you could see him sometimes, playing with him. He feeds him, changes him. I'm sure he loves him . . . loves us, I mean. I'm sure he does."

Heaven help us, thought Mary. She is infatuated with him still, the poor little fool. She felt choked with conflicting understanding and exasperation. She knew these two Roberts too well not to sympathise with Leonie's confusion. I've often regretted that I am his sister, she thought, but thank God I am not his mistress. What would she feel if Barrie treated her in this manner? Would it instantly kill the bond between them? Maybe not. She looked at Leonie with a new compassion.

"It's not myself I mind about," she was saying with pathetic sincerity. "I'm so frightened for Toby. He goes to him straight away when he has been drinking and picks him up no matter how late it is, even when he's asleep. I think he does it because he knows it upsets me more than anything," she added with sudden insight. "He knows I'm terrified that he will harm the baby. And he will, Mary. I know he will. Toby seems to sense it when he's drunk. I suppose it is the way he holds him – and then he cries and wriggles and tries to break away. I think that's what maddens Robert most. That the baby knows he is drunk and doesn't trust him.

"He took him up on deck one night – oh, a day or two ago. It was dark and I thought . . . oh, Mary, I thought he was going to throw him over. I know it sounds impossible, but if you had seen him. It is as if he had gone wild, and everything I say makes him wilder. And tonight. It's so foggy and black up there. Nobody would see, and I could do nothing to stop him. What shall I do, Mary? What shall I do?"

Mary sat silent for a moment. She felt as if she was floundering through some unspeakable nightmare. The idea that your own brother was capable of flinging a baby into a river should be unbelievable, preposterous. But she knew it was not preposterous. She had lived too long with Robert's rages, had seen too often the results of his violence, of his sudden shattering lack of control. Something seemed to crack in Robert that remained fast in ordinary people. It was like brake failure in a car; some quality that should, in the last resort, have stopped him, simply was not there. As a child he used to throw things through the window. She remembered the breaking glass, his flushed contorted face, the sad smashed toys on the pavement below. That nursery kitten – no, that she refused to remember; but the flash of recollection, the shadow of the old suspicion, decided her all the same.

"I think you'd better leave," she said, trying to keep her voice matter-of-fact, steady. "Just for a day or two, anyway. Clear off for a bit; give him time to sober up and get over it." Leonie was looking stricken. I have got to make her go, she thought in sudden desperation. I cannot leave her here with Robert. The dimly lit barge, the blanketing fog outside, were beginning to feel sinister, claustrophobic. She felt they were in a trap, and Robert, drunkenly returning, would be the successful trapper.

"You must go," she said urgently. "Now. I'll help you pack your things. You won't need much, and we can bundle Toby up in a blanket."

"But where will I go?" cried Leonie, backing away from her. "I don't know anyone round here, and I have no money. Where can I go like this, at night, with the baby?"

Mary looked at her as she stood in front of the cot; bullied, misused, ill treated, another piece of Robert's handiwork. Her long hair hung down like a curtain, and the wild dark eyes staring through it made her look like an injured animal defending its nest. Mary turned away; despite herself, she felt an unwelcome twinge of sympathy for Robert. This tendency to shrink and cower, the way she always looked hunted, martyred, she could well understand how such a manner had fed his natural leaning towards violence. We are to blame, she reflected guiltily. After all, we are his family. We should have seen this coming, done something to prevent it. When have we ever faced this hideous flaw in Robert? Even Father made himself blind to it. We have all indulged him, made excuses, and now we can't evade it any longer.

She glanced back at the girl with resignation and pity. She's our responsibility, she thought bitterly, Stella's and mine.

"You'd best come home with me," she said with authority. "There is plenty of room there. You'll be quiet and comfortable. And Robert won't think of you coming to us either; he doesn't even know I am here tonight."

All at once it seemed terribly important to hurry. She felt panic rising in her chest, singing in her eardrums. What if Robert came back and found them preparing to leave him? She thought again of the kitten, and of the dark oily water.

"I'm going to get a taxi," she said briskly, as if the whole thing was settled. "You go and pack while I use the telephone."

As she picked up the receiver the image of Barrie came to her, solid and reassuring, like a familiar landmark in a storm. Almost without volition she found she was dialling his number, and he answered immediately, before she had time to reconsider the automatic action. He must be at his desk, working at his brief, she thought, and I have disturbed him; but for once she did not care what he thought of her, it was so good to hear his voice.

"Barrie," she said, "it's Mary. I'm still on the barge at Chiswick." She hesitated, reluctant to betray Robert even to Barrie. "There's . . . there's been some trouble here," she went on. "Things have gone wrong – I'll explain it later. I've got to get Leonie off the boat tonight. Leonie and the baby."

She could feel her voice rising and paused to collect herself. I sound hysterical, she thought, ashamed. And what do I want him to do anyway? Why should he come all the way out here when I only have to call a taxi? 'I need you,' she wanted to say. 'I need you here, now, to dispel this horrible sensation of nightmare.' But the words would not come. She had never told Barrie that she needed him. She must not do so now.

"Mary?" he was saying. "Mary, what's the matter?" He was jiggling the receiver rest as if he thought they had been cut off. "Are you still there?" he shouted.

"Could you come? Could you come and collect us?" she said, regretting now that she had been so weak as to bother him. "I'm sorry, Barrie, I know you are very busy, but it's dreadful down here and they are hurt – Leonie and the baby. I just thought if you could possibly. . ."

"Of course I'll come," he cut in sharply. "I'll be there as soon as I can make it. The fog looks heavy, but the roads should be fairly clear."

"Thank you," she said weakly, amazed that her relief was so enormous. It would be all right once Barrie was with them. But how long will he be, she wondered. Will Robert get here before him?

"Hurry," she added involuntarily. "Hurry, Barrie. I'm really frightened." She tried a laugh to soften the words, but even to herself it sounded strained and peculiar.

"Right!" he said abruptly. "I'll leave directly. Keep your heart up, golliwog."

The line went dead and she stared at the crackling receiver. Somewhere in the background Leonie was dropping her belongings. Why don't they get stronger light bulbs, she thought crossly. No wonder she breaks things, the place is a mass of shadows. She felt a strong disinclination to leave the telephone; it seemed her only link with sanity this evening. But she replaced the receiver resolutely. She'll be all night packing if I don't help her, she thought nervously. Toby will need things, and we must be ready to go.

In fact it did not take long to gather Leonie's belongings together. There seemed pathetically few of them. And what there are, are none too clean, thought Mary, disgustedly stuffing a duffle bag in the dismal cabin. She had not been into the sleeping quarters since Leonie had moved in, and looking round at the squalid mess she wondered again how Robert could endure it. He had always been fastidious in his person, and his room at home had been clean even if it was sometimes untidy. Now, looking at the unmade bed, the grimy sheets, the piles of used tissues, she realised how much he must have changed since he started to live with Leonie. What had happened to his self-respect? Why was he drinking so heavily? And it must be very heavy indeed, thought Mary, for him to put up with this sordidness. The old Robert would have fallen on it with rage and repugnance and shovelled most of it into a dust-bin.

"Let's go and sit down," she said, averting her eyes from what seemed to be a pile of used nappies in the corner. "I think we're about finished."

She had known that the waiting would seem interminable, but it was even worse than she had feared. The thought of Robert was becoming monstrous to her; she could almost see him lurching round the corner of the stairwell. Leonie sat as if paralysed, holding the baby in her arms. She had wrapped him tightly in a matted woolly blanket and he looked stiff and uncomfortable, but he slept as though he were drugged – or drowned, thought Mary uncontrollably. She almost wished he would wake and make a racket, the silence was so uncanny. It seemed fatuous to talk to Leonie, who was obviously past replying, and they sat speechless, united in their apprehension, listening to the eerie creaking of the barge.

When the footfalls came, they shot to their feet together, as if charged by the same electric current, but the steps were heavy and deliberate. Mary knew at once that they were Barrie's. She flew up the stairs and flung herself against him, struggling to suppress her sudden humiliating tears. He seemed out of breath and his coat and hair were beaded with damp from the fog; she felt she had never been so glad to see anyone.

"I thought you'd never get here," she said shakily, taking his hand and pulling him down to the cabin. "We've got to get going as quick as we can."

"You sound as if the boat is sinking," said Barrie cheerfully. "And where are we taking them in such a hurry? I hope it's not to a hospital?" He did not sound concerned; in fact, he sounded positively festive, as if he had just arrived at a party. He is relieved I am all right, thought Mary with sudden pleasure. He has been really worried about me.

The baby had started to cry at last and Leonie was coming towards them, dragging her ill-assorted luggage through the litter on the floor. Barrie was regarding them with amazement; they certainly looked pretty unappetising.

"It's worse than that," she said light-headedly, laughing for the first time that evening. "So bad I hardly like to tell you. I've asked them to come and stay with us. We are going to take them home."

# 5

There was a menace somewhere, drifting darkly in and out of her awareness, threatening the rapture of the movement that carried her so effortlessly across the smooth ice. She would ignore it; she would let nothing spoil this freedom, this intoxicating weightlessness. She was floating. Flying. Nothing must stop her now. If she could just go on gliding like this, she would be impervious to everything; to danger, to horror, to the cold that was somehow making her lighter, smaller, so that she blew before the glacial wind, brittle and frosted like a dried leaf.

But suddenly, discordantly, she could see the children. She did not want to see the children. She would not see them. She spun, glided away from them; from hostile unresponsive Mary, always baffling, always frustratingly out of reach, and from Robert who exhausted and sapped her, draining her emotions like a leech.

He was only a baby today, she noticed without surprise, and Mary was bending over him protectively, her plaits sticking up in the air. She knew from the way they were moving that they could not see her, did not know she was there. Today she was free, invisible; and today, though they looked so lost and vulnerable, they would not trap her.

She whirled away from them, seeking to recapture the liquid delight of the freedom, knowing as she turned that the joy was gone, that the threat was nearer. She swept towards it, round it, away from it. Her movements had become frenzied, chaotic, beyond her control. Beneath her feet the ice was cracking, crazily cracking in all directions, splintering like a shattered windscreen. Gashes of blackness were appearing, multiplying with remorseless finality, snaking towards the place where she had lost sight of the children, the place where she knew she had left them to perish. She could not reach them.

She could not see them; the cold was paralysing, blinding her. They would be swallowed, engulfed in the deathly blackness.

"Mary!" screamed Stella in agony, "Mary! Robert! Where are you? Where are you?"

She woke with the scream in her throat and her arms flung out rigid before her. She was shaking uncontrollably with terror and cold. Her hands were numb and unresponsive and she pulled herself up in bed clumsily, fumbling for the lamp. Even as a child she had not feared the dark, had never scrabbled frantically, hysterically towards the light as she found herself doing now. The relief, as her fingers found the switch, shamed and overwhelmed her. She fell back on the pillows, exhausted by the effort, disgusted with her fear and her weakness, defiled even by the clammy sweat that trickled from her body onto the clean linen of her bed.

They were indecent, these nightmares. They made the nights, already a trial of discomfort and sleeplessness, into an almost intolerable ordeal, and here particularly, she felt unequal to the challenge; she had always slept soundly, serenely. She had allowed nothing to disturb her, had taken a pride in her ability to pack away her worries and responsibilities and return to her work each day, refreshed. Even during that brief nursery period she had not allowed the pattern to be interrupted. It had been Henry who woke when the children cried. Henry who had turned on lights, soothed them, dealt with their bad dreams and fears of the darkness. And if sometimes he lay anxious and awake, he never mentioned it, thought Stella guiltily, looking round the pleasant faded room where more than anywhere else she still felt close to Henry. Perhaps he knew how little understanding I had of the sleepless. Insomnia was something I always felt a determined nature should be able to control. I remember saying something of the kind to Julia; that sleeplessness was a problem of the inadequate, that the self-disciplined seldom suffered from insomnia. Insomnia. Such an ugly word, with its overtones of neurosis, its whiff of despair. Perhaps that's why I avoided really thinking about it. I avoided anything that I found ugly and distasteful. Like the distress I found in Julia.

Appalled, her mind skidded away from the thought. No. Not Julia. Surely I did not avoid her, did not turn away from Julia? I tried to cheer her up, to keep her from brooding. I asked her to parties, took her to exhibitions, introduced her to new friends. I did not avoid Julia.

She sat up in bed gingerly, easing the ache in her breast, and poured herself some milk from the thermos beside her.

Everyone had said how good she was to Julia; how she had done everything she could to help her. Everyone had respected her reluctance to speak of Julia after she had died. It was widely known how close they had been. No one had suspected that she did not speak of Julia simply because she was not thinking of Julia, that she had resolutely expunged such a disturbing memory of misery from her life.

Stella stared at the milk, at the fragile wrinkled skin that was forming on its surface. And yet we were close to each other, she thought, Julia and I. We gave each other such a lot; laughter, companionship, stimulation – all sorts of happy things. It worked all right while it was a two-way traffic; but what did I give you back, Julia, when instead of laughter you brought me your sorrow, when it was not your enthusiasm you asked me to share, but your despair? Did I let you talk about it at all, your loss, your emptiness, your sleeplessness? Did I try to understand, to concern myself with your embarrassing distress? Compassion; that was all you asked of me. Not the trite brisk sympathy I gave, but compassion, the true involvement of loving friendship.

She shivered, drawing the quilt tighter about her shoulders. Julia used to huddle so, she remembered, and she had told her she should eat more, get proper exercise.

"I gave you nothing," she said aloud, face to face suddenly with that huddled Julia. Oh, I know I talked to you, talked about everything under the sun that passed inspection as a healthy subject for conversation, 'lifting your mind' I called it. 'Julia, you must lift your mind. You are young, intelligent, you have talent. Don't sit there moping. Why not come with us tonight, for instance? It's bound to be an interesting crowd.' And then you would come, and because you were proud, you stopped attempting to engulf me in your unhappiness, in your panic, in your ugly insomnia. I loved you again then, for a little, because of your bravery, because of your pride. 'Julia's getting over it,' I said. 'I knew she would. It was just a matter of getting her to lift her mind.'

She closed her eyes, struggling to face the old self-deception. It was clear to her now, subconsciously she had always known, that Julia's suicide had been no sudden brainstorm. All the signals had been there if she had been prepared to read them. What she had dismissed as unpredictable had been a perfectly logical turn of events. She had considered Julia better because she wanted her better; she had assumed her pathetic façade of recovery to be real because it suited her to do so; she had refused to admit that her friend was still tormented and bewildered, edging towards the point where self-destruction seemed the only answer.

She must face it now; she must put it into words. I helped to kill you, Julia, because I could not, no, because I would not, let the sane flow of my own life be disrupted.

She put down the untasted milk. She was totally culpable; she stood condemned of the worst sort of selfishness. She felt shaken and yet curiously purged by the confession. Have I always withheld myself, she wondered? Is there any point where I have given myself freely, without baulking at the cost?

To Henry? It would be comforting to think so, but to regard any need of Henry's as an opportunity for generosity would be wholly false. By the time Henry had needed her compassion he was simply part of herself. His illness, his pain, his death even, had been in a fashion her own. It had required no sacrifice, no act of will, to throw herself into his struggle, for it was by definition her struggle too. She had fought with him for his life, totally committed to his need of her, but their needs had been complementary, and the life for which she was fighting was the life that they had come to share.

It angered her still to think of those letters of condolence that suggested the gratification she should draw from the thought of her own care and devotion during his illness. They implied that through ill health Henry had become a burden, nobly carried and thankfully put down. Surely nobody who had experienced real affection could write in such a vein? They would have known it was impossible for her to behave unselfishly towards Henry, who through love had become part of her very being.

No, she thought, firmly pursuing the horrible clarity of the memory. No. I was just as self-engrossed as ever. It was towards Mary that I should have tried to direct my sympathy. I should have made the effort to comfort her, to be tender towards her. I should not have been wholly absorbed in my concern for Henry. I should have found the strength to be of more support to her in her shock and grief.

She could see Mary now, her shoulders bowed over the book before her, sitting beside her father's bed. She had read to him heroically, long after he had become too ill to concentrate on her voice, or the meaning of the words she spoke. They both knew that it would have been painful for him to admit that his mind was no longer active, and they did not mention it to each other either, but read on doggedly, determined to ignore the growing listlessness in his eyes.

Yes, how absolutely in tune she had been, both through those months of crisis and in the unearthly aftermath of Henry's death. During that dreadful year even Robert had grated upon her, she remembered; but never Mary.

I must tell her, she thought suddenly. I'm sure I never thanked her. I must tell her how much she meant to me, how completely I relied on her understanding and tact.

Borne along by the strength of the impulse, she swung her legs out of bed before she realised what she was doing. Now standing unsteadily by her table she noticed the clock, and saw that it would be impossible to seek Mary out at such an hour, however good the reason. No one could be expected to be pleased at being wakened for a chat at two o'clock in the morning. She sighed in frustration, dully aware that there would be no more sleep that night. It was always fatal now, this waking in the small hours, her mind obsessed with failure and fear. And there were five more hours to put in before she could decently call the night over. I must try to relax, she told herself, sitting rigid with cold and discomfort on the edge of the mattress. If I do not rest I shall never finish the bird.

Her book had fallen to the floor and she sank wearily to her knees to reach it. It was then, with her hand stretched out and her head half under the bed that the amazing noise first came to her, startling her abruptly into her day-time self. Robert! was her first instinctive thought, but the day-time self dismissed it instantly. Robert was a grown man now, however he appeared in her dreams. Yet she was sure, as sure as the drugs allowed her to be of anything, that the sound she had heard was the sound of a baby, a loud, indignant sound, unmistakably a baby's cry.

I must be going mad, she thought distractedly, but she sat back on her heels, alert and listening.

Yes, there it was again, directly above her. Impossible though it was, a baby was certainly crying here and now, in her own house, a few feet above her head.

Suddenly she felt absurdly invigorated. What an unexpected diversion! And how welcome, coming in the middle of what threatened to be a particularly depressing and endless night. Perhaps life as she had loved it, with all its intriguing small mysteries and surprises, was not quite over after all.

Spurred by a new energy she belted her dressing-gown, found her slippers, and stepped lightly into the passage.

The stairs presented a momentary set back. How she had grown to detest staircases! Here in this thin, terraced house they were an ever-present hazard. There always seemed to be one, sharp and steep, lying between her and where she wanted to be. Sometimes she almost felt the things were alive, lurking about in the shadows ready to remind her of her weakness if she should for a moment manage to forget it.

When the children were small, they used to play games with the stairs. Could they take them four at a time? How many flights without drawing a breath? Now in her frailty she found herself doing the same. Would she have to rest on the half-landing? Could she get to the return without her lungs fighting for air? Each staircase was becoming an individual enemy, with its own particular weapon of attack.

The one that led to the first floor, to her bedroom and the

studio, was the most difficult to combat, for each ounce of strength it won from her was strength that should have been devoted to her carving. She felt it had unfair advantage in the battle since it always attacked her when she most wanted to conserve her energy. It was no longer a question of whether it would win, but of how great or small would be its victory.

On the other hand, the broad steps from the street to the hall door, which she had once regarded with disdain, had now become an unexpected menace. True, the flight was short, but its strength lay in the cunning nature of its position. Not only did it catch you as you came home, usually at your lowest ebb and with the need for rest at its most pressing, but it also exposed your every weakness to the full view of the passers-by. Lately, since this appalling cough had arisen to plague her, she had found herself terrified of being unmasked completely. You could hardly sink to the ground outside your own front door, or even lean on the railings gasping for breath, without exciting attention. Those giddy blurred moments spent struggling to unite key and lock were fast becoming insupportable. One day she would collapse, in public, practically on the pavement. The outside steps were winning, fresh strategy was called for. Now, looking with dislike at the steep staircase that led to the upper landing, it came to her suddenly that a garden seat was the answer. At right angles to the house, with its back to the railings, it would not look incongruous. I shall put a pot plant on the other side so that I have something pleasant to look at while I cough, she thought with satisfaction. First round to me.

The house seemed ominously silent now. She climbed slowly, husbanding her energy, listening anxiously for some fresh evidence that a baby was above her.

It was so quiet; she began to wonder bleakly whether her senses were indeed beginning to fail her and that she might find that she had imagined the whole thing. But no. As she rounded the return of the stairwell she saw with relief that she had not been mistaken. Her spare room, which should have been empty, was definitely occupied; a crack of light was showing brightly through the gap where the embrasure met the door.

For the first time she hesitated, would there be someone with the baby? It would hardly be all alone. Well, whoever it was they had abrogated any right to privacy by arriving uninvited in the middle of the night. Had there been a keyhole she would unashamedly have put her eye to it, but unfortunately there was none. She opened the door as quietly as she could and peered eagerly inside.

The confusion which met her eyes startled her for a moment. Although she had prepared herself for a baby, she had some-how pictured it without trappings, lying in a carrycot perhaps, but with the neat pretty room unchanged around it. Now, as her glance took in the open suitcases, the scatter of nappies, the tins of milk, the rolls of cotton wool, she realised she had forgotten most of the paraphernalia of the nursery. Two duffle bags had been shaken empty on the bed beside her, disgorging a haphazard mountain of garments and foodstuffs, and the table was covered with an unpleasing selection of bottles and teats. An extraordinary amount of tissues were scattered in all directions, as though a brisk wind had blown them hither and thither about the room, and on the carpet at her feet someone had spilt a tin of talcum powder.

She recoiled in distaste, offended by the wildness of the disorder. There was something not quite right about such unrestrained untidiness, as if the person who had unpacked was distraught or unstable. And where was her visitor? There was no one in the room, unless they were hiding. For the first time she felt a twinge of uneasiness. It was not natural to fling things about in this manner, and she could not help noticing that the clothes themselves looked grubby and uncared for. Indeed the room had acquired an air of hysteria that was undoubtedly disturbing. She felt foolish and helpless, like a child disappointed in a forbidden game that he knows he should never have started. In the messy room the feeling of pleasant adventure had evaporated, the excitement gone sour. She had almost forgotten the baby itself in her contemplation of the chaos around her, and now she found that her curiosity had gone cold.

I'd better wake Mary, she decided reluctantly. I'm no match

for a deranged squatter in the state I'm in nowadays.

The thought was a worrying one; she hoped Mary would not notice anything strange about her appearance, for she knew how ill she had begun to look at night. However, there seemed nothing else to be done. She would just have to risk it.

Her mind made up, she turned again to the doorway and came face to face with a girl standing uncertainly on the threshold. In one hand she carried a steaming saucepan, from which protruded the top of a feeding bottle. Her face appeared to be exceedingly dirty, and she carried her other arm in a sling.

# 6

Startled by the sight of each other, Stella and the girl stood mesmerised, motionless and staring in the dim lamp-light.

To Stella, fogged with drugs and weariness, this new apparition seemed perfectly fitting. In the sense of unreality that pervaded the night the ghostly girl, so pale and still, was surely not incongruous. She felt no impulse to break the silence that grew restfully between them, and it was the girl who spoke first, though her voice, gentle and unemphatic, scarcely troubled the illusion of a dream.

"I had to warm some milk for the baby," she said simply, as if that explained everything in a satisfactory manner. "I brought up one of your saucepans. I hope you don't mind?"

She crossed the room as she spoke and clumsily lowered the pan and bottle to the bedside table.

"Of course not," said Stella politely. Her gaze drifted to the steaming bottle and a shadow of the day-time self stirred within her. She moved rapidly towards it and slipped a magazine under the hot metal. It will make a ring on the polish, she thought dazedly; how trying the young can be.

The brisk movement brought a giddiness that dismayed her, and she sat down hastily on the untidy bed. "Of course not," she repeated vaguely, concentrating on subduing the dizziness before it got the better of her. "I heard the baby crying. Of course it must be fed."

Really, she felt little curiosity now about this dream-like guest whose quiet manner was so soothing and harmonious, and she was almost sorry when she heard her speak again.

"My name is Leonie," she was saying slowly, as if it was a struggle to recall the information, "and my baby, he's . . . he's called Toby." She indicated the far side of the room, and for the first time Stella, following the gesture, saw the carrycot in the shadow on the window seat, half hidden by the heavy curtain drawn against the night.

"He's a good baby," the girl was saying proudly. "He had a fall yesterday and he's muddled by the moving most likely. But he hardly cries when he's well, you know. He hardly cries at all."

"I'm glad to hear that," said Stella wryly. The light-headedness was ebbing, and the girl looked at her anxiously, hearing the edge on her voice, suddenly aware that perhaps there was more to be explained.

"I'm a friend of Robert's," she said at last. For the first time she sounded uneasy, unsure of her ground.

A friend of Robert's. She did not look like one of Robert's friends. On the whole they tended to be confident, cock-sure, you might be tempted to say. She had usually found the girls particularly brash, with a veneer of sophistication that was completely lacking in the forlorn waif before her.

"Did Robert bring you, then?" she asked, as the girl seemed unwilling to continue. "Is he here now?"

Leonie turned away from her, rubbing the sling as if it irritated her. "He doesn't know I'm here," she said woodenly. "It was Mary who brought us."

"Mary?" said Stella, astonished. Somehow she had not considered Mary as part of their weird situation. Why Mary? she thought in bewilderment. How unlike Mary to get mixed up in one of Robert's dilemmas. It was quite out of character.

"You say that Mary brought you?" she asked again. Her voice sounded sharp suddenly, interrogative and demanding. Leonie stared at her warily, the easy acceptance that had been between them shattered at last.

"She said you wouldn't mind," she said after a pause, and added nervously, "we'd both been hurt, you see. We had an accident."

"An accident?" echoed Stella foolishly. She stared at the girl. Yes, she looked as if she had been in an accident all right. But even allowing for shock there was something faintly strange in the way she spoke about Robert. What was it she had said? 'He doesn't know I'm here.' Why not? Had Robert been in the accident too? Was he injured?

Shocking, violent, the old horror flashed into her mind. The screaming brakes, the twisted car, the sirens and the shouting. And Robert, Robert. It was one of the worst nightmares, the most recurrent, the most realistic. In panic and terror, she fairly flung herself at Leonie.

"Where is Robert?" she cried urgently. "Why is he not with you?" The girl's remoteness no longer seemed appealing; it was infuriating, intolerable. Robert had been hurt, was maimed, dead perhaps, and no one had the courage to tell her.

"Why is he not with you?" she repeated wildly, her voice rising in the fury of her anxiety. "Why don't you answer me? What has happened to Robert?"

But Leonie shrank away from her like a phantom, mute and insubstantial, and it was Mary's voice that answered her, blessedly sane and familiar, in a room that seemed to be reeling around her.

"Robert's all right, Stella," said Mary from the doorway. "What on earth are you making this fuss about? Nothing has happened to Robert."

With her back to Mary, Stella shut her eyes. Robert was alive. Robert was well. Nothing had happened to Robert. Mary was here, and everything was real again. Normal. How can I have been so foolish and uncontrolled? she thought angrily. Frightening the girl, waking Mary . . . making a spectacle of myself? Still, she had to admit that her legs were weak, her head light with relief, her heart pounding. Nothing had happened to Robert.

She opened her eyes as she felt Mary's hand on her shoulder. She looked troubled and underslept, Stella noticed, and her face was full of concern. "What's the matter with you?" she was saying gently. "Don't you hear me? Is something wrong?"

What do I say? thought Stella hopelessly. 'Mary, I'm dying. I'm riddled with cancer, poisoned with drugs; I can't sleep and I'm losing control of my actions'?

She lifted her face; they were so seldom physically close like this, but now their cheeks were almost touching. She had forgotten how poignant Mary's eyes would be at close quarters. Wide grey eyes, darkened by the size of the pupils, vulnerable and expressive. Henry's eyes. Now she read the anxiety in them as one reads a familiar phrase in a language all but forgotten, and her heart lurched at the memory. Henry's eyes. Mary's eyes. How could she keep them empty of pain and worry? I cannot do this to her, she thought. Not now. Not for a little. Somehow I must protect her from it.

She looked away, straightening her shoulders, and walked across the room to the window. She felt she would breathe more evenly away from the girls and their overpowering closeness, away from the lamplight, away from Henry's eyes.

"I'm sorry," she said as lightly as she could. "Leonie told me she had been in an accident and I'm afraid I assumed that it had involved Robert. As he wasn't here I thought that he'd been . . . well, that he had been hurt badly." She paused; she was getting into her stride now. How tiresome that she had given in to her fear for Robert. "I must add that Leonie did nothing to reassure me," she concluded crisply. "I would have thought she might have had the kindness to tell me that my son was unhurt."

"I hardly think that kindness is a quality that this family should expect from anybody," said Mary acidly; and Stella, hearing with relief the coldness in her voice, knew that for the moment at least she had dispelled the concern.

"As for Robert," Mary went on grimly, 'I'm beginning to think that a car accident would be about the best thing that could happen to Robert. He's not safe to have around, he should be shut away. And if it's going to be a choice between a gaol and a hospital, then a few broken bones might save us a lot of embarrassment."

Stella regarded her calmly. She was used to Mary's outbursts about Robert; she hardly listened to them any more. But I must prepare myself to listen to a fresh iniquity, she thought with reluctance. Something bad must have provoked such an impassioned attack.

She had addressed the question to Mary, but Leonie cut in abruptly. For the first time she seemed jolted out of her apathy, and she rounded on Mary with a look that was almost one of anger.

"You shouldn't speak of Robert like that," she said. "It's terrible to say such things about him. You don't know anything about it anyway – you weren't even there when it happened."

She turned to Stella and went on hurriedly. "He was very drunk," she said. "He'd never have done it if he had been sober. He loves the baby, you know, and there's no reason why he should, really. He could have been . . . well . . . so different."

Stella looked at her with irritation. The girl was incoherent; she had not answered the question. What had Robert actually done, so awful that he would not have contemplated it sober? Nonetheless, she found herself reluctantly touched by Leonie's tone, recognising the lame defensiveness that had so often been her own. And the baby, whom Robert loved, but about whom he could have felt quite otherwise?

A new thought struck her, more exhilarating than alarming, and she turned to the carrycot without speaking and peered inside.

The baby lay sleeping. She was glad that Leonie had warned her that he had been injured, but even so she winced at the sight of the swollen face and the bandages. Despite them though, she saw he looked placid and contented; a fat, dimpled baby – fair, with straight blonde hair. The dark curls were not there, nor the high cheek-bones and wiry energetic frame that she had been half expecting. It was not Robert's baby.

She was astonished at her disappointment. Surely she had not hoped. . .? But yes, it would have been thrilling, fulfilling somehow, to have seen Robert's child. How absurd I am, she thought, crossly; it must be the drugs, this endless fever. She straightened her back, putting the ridiculous thought behind her, and met Leonie's gaze where she stood at the head of the cot.

"No," the girl said softly. She sounds sorry for me, thought Stella. Are my very thoughts becoming naked? "No, he's not Robert's baby."

And as Stella paused, uncertain how to reply to the unspoken sympathy, she added almost wistfully, "He'd never have done this if Toby had been his own child – never! It's very hard for him, surely you can see that? It wouldn't be the same if Toby was his. . ."

As the truth came to Stella, she was aware of a new and curious sensation. It was as though she were outside her body. Above it somewhere. She could see the shock-waves running through it, radiating from a middle point around the heart outwards, like the ripples made by a stone thrown into a pond. She could tell, too, that close to the base of the skull the vibrations were in trouble. Dimly, she sensed that the earth-bound, far-away Stella was experiencing pain in that connection, as if the ripples had piled up at some unexpected barrier, causing insupportable pressure at the top of her neck.

Looking down on the scene with detached and impersonal interest she realised that if the pressure found no outlet the result would be disastrous. Something vital was being strained, stretched taut, threatened with breaking-point. But the crisis could hardly hold her attention; she was far above it all. It was only annoying to feel that she could not desert that other Stella entirely, that she must hang around to see what happened to her. She would not be kept waiting long, though, to judge by the throbbing of the mounting pressure. The decisive moment was almost there.

One last blow. It was like those coloured balloons she used to inflate for the children. Robert had always wanted them bigger. 'Harder!' he used to cry, pink in the face and hopping on one leg in excitement. 'Blow harder!' And Stella, gasping and laughing, would puff on until she reached the critical point – one more blow. Would she get away with it this time? Would the glistening rubber sphere be perfected, the knot triumphantly tied? Or would this last gambler's throw blast the whole thing into nothing?

Mary used to run behind her Father with her hands clapped over her ears. Stella remembered how she would implore him to stop them, tears of nervous apprehension in her eyes. But they were recklessly united, she and the prancing, shouting

68

Robert. They ignored all protest, pitiless in their determination, drawn by the lure of that final, unpredictable, crucial blow.

There! They had done it again. Their luck had held; the pressure was receding. On the instant, without effort, the two Stellas had become one. Only the icy coldness of her hands and feet and the numbness at the back of her neck were left to remind her that anything unusual had happened.

She put her hand uncertainly to the point where the pressure had been, easing her head from side to side to loosen the tension in the muscles, almost surprised that they still seemed to be in working order. Her eyes too were functioning normally, and she blinked them quickly to try to improve the focus. Yes, here was the familiar room with its unfamiliar litter; the saucepan still steaming on the table; the baby still sleeping in the carrycot. And the two girls, incredibly they seemed to have noticed nothing. Leonie was standing protectively by the head of the crib, just as she had been when she had last seen her. Mary, on the other side of the bed, was speaking loudly and rudely, in a harsh unpleasing voice that jarred on the ear. I hope she doesn't wake the baby, thought Stella, still a little bewildered. I wonder why she sounds so angry?

But of course! She knew why Mary was angry. It was because of Robert. Robert had finally done something wholly unforgivable; had injured this harmless girl who appeared to be fond of him; had beaten or battered a tiny helpless baby. How monstrous. How shocking.

But this time the words were empty of meaning; the truth had lost its impact, its power to horrify. It was as if the experiences of the last few moments had purged her alike of surprise and anger, as though she had used up her capacity to feel shock. All she could see was that child who had been Robert, dancing round her drunk with his wild vitality, compulsively pushing his luck . . . pushing his luck.

Reluctantly she tore her eyes from the vision and looked instead at Mary. Mary, who was satisfied with half-sized balloons; who always behaved properly and sanely. What was she saying in that self-righteous voice of hers? That this time

Robert had gone too far; that they should withdraw all support from him; desert him; betray him; run him in to the police. That he was vicious. Dangerous.

Robert! How absurd to speak this way of him. How disgusting to suggest such unthinkable things before a stranger. Mary should be old enough to realise that there must be some adequate explanation for this distressing situation. Certainly Robert was moody, volatile; there was no doubt he had a quick temper, that he was drinking too much lately, but for Mary to try and turn him into a monster was preposterous. She must be stopped at once; the girl was clearly overwrought.

"You are talking nonsense, Mary," she said with icy restraint, as if to the difficult child who had occasionally overstepped herself in the early years of her marriage. "It is clear to me that you do not know what you are saying. I suggest you get some sleep, and in the morning you will see the matter more clearly."

She turned to Leonie, refusing to be stricken by Mary's stony face. "The bottle is getting cold," she said. "You had better feed your baby." She smiled at her visitor, feeling calm and reasonable. "I shall go to bed myself," she added. "We can discuss matters tomorrow, when we are all less exhausted."

Her legs seemed very far away, but she was pleased to find she could move them without difficulty. Erect and dignified, satisfied with her command of the situation, she passed slowly between the two silent girls and left the room.

# 7

Mary could hear the telephone ringing before she reached the door of her office. She ran the last few yards and snatched up the receiver, wedging it awkwardly between chin and chest while she dumped her bag and file and the armful of morning mail haphazardly on the desk.

"Mary Leonard," she said abruptly, annoyed to find that she was out of breath. Bad enough to be late for work without advertising the fact to an early morning caller; especially when she always made such a point of punctuality. She could hardly remember another time when she had arrived half-an-hour late for the office.

"Oh Mary! Gay here," said the voice at the other end of the receiver. "Glad you've made it in time for tea-break! C.D. wants you in his office. I've been calling you all morning."

She recognised the tone with a sinking heart. Gay's voice sounded smug and faintly triumphant. It was obvious that she was under no illusion as to why Mary's phone had remained unanswered, which was a pity, as Gay was reputed to have a good deal of influence on Cecil Davies, besides being his secretary.

C.D. was important; one of the Directors, boss of her immediate superior; Head of the Department. Account Executives did not care to keep him waiting. He was shrewd and unscrupulous, an impulsive and sometimes inaccurate judge of character, and Mary knew that his patronage was uncertain; she had sometimes seen it withdrawn with alarming speed. So far, she had got on well with him. She had even begun to trust him, to hope that he liked her. Certainly he had been influential in getting her the Barratts account. And little I've done to confirm his judgement, thought Mary. Blast Robert. Blast Stella.

"Tell him I'll be along directly," she said. "Sorry to have

kept him waiting." She put down the telephone hastily, swallowing the impulse to invent a good reason for her empty office. Really, it was shaming, to be so humbled by the thought of an impatient C.D.

C.D.! Stella always laughed at the way Markhams referred to their senior executives by initial. And it is ridiculous, thought Mary. It's just an affectation of importance. After all, there was a clerk in Stationery called Christopher Donnan, but everyone would think Chris mad if he presumed to use his initials, in Markhams they could mean nothing but Cecil Davies: the great, the one-and-only C.D.

Her eyes fell to the memo on top of her in-tray. 'From E.N.T. to Mary Leonard,' advising her that her market research estimates were way out by Media Department reckoning. Edward Norman Thompson, Chief Media Statistician, E.N.T. She had never got on well with Eddie, and it did put him in perspective to recall that Stella believed, or feigned to believe, that he was a failed Ear, Nose and Throat Specialist. "Poor man," she would say vaguely, in answer to Mary's furious grumbling, "I expect he finds difficulty in adjusting to life outside the hospital." It was cheering to think how irritated Eddie would be to hear himself dismissed like that. Even if it irked sometimes to have her whole working life dismissed as a puerility, it was good to have Stella around, deflating the pompous, refusing to take the trivial seriously.

But now, stepping into C.D.'s office – "Go on in, Mary," Gay had said ominously in the ante-room. "He's been wondering what's keeping you." – she realised that the thought of Stella must be blotted out immediately. She must not think of her extraordinary behaviour last night, of her irresponsibility towards Robert, nor above all of those horrible bottles, still unexplained, still leaden at the back of her consciousness. She must have a clear mind if she was to be a match for Cecil this morning.

He sat on his swivel chair, his back half turned to the room, gazing out over the Aldwych. He did not swing round – a bad sign – but continued looking out of the window, apparently absorbed in the doings of some pigeons on the opposite parapet.

Mary clenched her jaw, determined not to feel diminished by a treatment she had witnessed so often, nor by the hugeness of the glistening desk and the acres of carpet she had to cross to reach it. That was C.D. all over; he had the whole office arranged to emphasise his own importance, to put the outsider at the maximum disadvantage. All those telephones, for instance; she had never seen him use more than two of them. She suspected the others were fakes. And the swivel chair, that was his major prop and he certainly knew how to use it. When he was bored or displeased he would rock it petulantly and restively like a baby, and the offending executive, put off by the noise and movement, would stutter into silence. But it was when he wished to show enthusiasm that it came into full flower. He would sit as he did now, staring out of the window, until the favoured client (or, much more rarely, the favoured executive) was half-way towards him. Then, as if startled out of a reverie, he would swing round in glad astonishment, leaping to his feet in his delight and leaving the chair flying round and round wildly behind him. The fact that you knew Gay had announced the caller minutes before did not stop it from being an effective performance of boyish exuberance. She had seen some of the most unapproachable clients fairly lap it up.

"Good morning, C.D.," she said now, rather loudly. There was nothing worse than having to repeat so banal a greeting. That had happened once at the beginning, when she had made the mistake of using a tone muted enough for him to ignore.

"Why, Mary!" He sounded surprised, as if he had long given up all hope of her answering his summons. "Nice of you to come along!"

He swung round painfully, as if he was stiff from waiting, and she saw with horror that he had all the Barratts files on the polished desk before him; the art work, the television campaign, her roughs for the new slogans, Eddie's figures on the market research estimates – everything. How had he got hold of them, she wondered stupidly; but of course he had only to get Gay to go round and collect the files from the relevant offices. No secretary would deny information to the great

C.D. Still, it was incredibly insulting of him, to have gone round gleaning information behind her back like this. It was her account now, and moreover he had given it to her; he only had to ask her and she would have brought the whole thing down to him in the appropriate manner. Anger stung her. Really, it was unheard of for him to interfere as early as this, and downright creepy to think of him going through her filing cabinet.

"I'm afraid Gay must have had quite a time collecting all my papers for you," she said frigidly. "What a pity she did not ask me for them! It would have saved her a lot of time."

"And been much more ethical too, you mean? Good for you, Mary." He looked up and surprisingly favoured her with one of his most ingenuous smiles. "As a matter of fact," he went on, "Gay had nothing to do with it. I collected all this myself, last night. About sixish. You must have scarpered fairly early. And the Barratts files, just for the record, they weren't in the cabinet. They were lying on the desk where you had left them."

"I only had to go burgling," he went on ruminatively, "to find the art work. Lord, what a mess there is in that studio! I haven't been up there for ages, I don't know how Roy puts up with it. Still, I found it in the end, and very good it is, if I may say so Mary. All your idea?"

She nodded and he gestured to a chair. "Well, sit down anyway and stop looking so outraged. I can see you think I have a lot of explaining to do."

He's being too nice, she thought gloomily. That always augurs badly.

"Last night," he was saying, "about sixish, as I told you, I had a personal phone call from Basil Barratt."

He paused for effect, and Mary carefully kept her face without expression, but her spirits fell lower. The Barratts still held a controlling interest in the family firm. Old Sir Graham was Chairman of its Board of Directors, and Basil Barratt, at present involving himself in the firm at all levels, was his only son. He had been at the meeting, with his publicity man beside him, and she felt he had not liked her; and no wonder, she thought, considering the show I put up yesterday.

"Well, anyway Mary," C.D. went on, "the gist of the call was that Basil Barratt wasn't happy. He was off to France this morning, trouble with the vineyards they own there, or something, and he felt he must speak to me before he left. He hadn't got much of a grasp of the campaign – well, it does look scrappy at this stage, and he's no authority on advertising, but he had been left with an unhappy impression at the meeting."

He paused with his elbows on the table and carefully put the tips of his fingers together. Here it comes, thought Mary.

"To put it baldly, he said you'd not inspired him with any confidence. He wanted me to know that in his opinion you did not seem capable of handling the job. He suggested I find someone more experienced for the account, who could bring, how did he put it exactly, a clearer head to the problems involved."

C.D. paused and looked at her, but she could not read his face. Bewilderment? Sympathy? Anger? What did it matter anyway? When a client asks for a change of executive, you presumably give him what he's demanding. It was the golden rule of advertising; please the client or lose the account.

"Oh?" she said, inadequately. She could think of nothing else to say.

"Well, to be honest," C.D. continued after a moment, "I could see what he was getting at. You weren't impressive at that meeting, Mary. In fact, if I had not seen you sitting before me I would have said you weren't there at all. And you looked as if you'd just come back from the moon or something."

He leant forward across the desk and glared at her aggressively.

"You were a *flop*, Mary. A disaster. And I can't afford flops in my department. You made all this excellent work," he tapped the files with the end of his gold pencil, "sound like so much bullshit. And the point is that it *is* excellent work. The ideas are good. The art work's good. Even the idea behind the market research is good, for all E.N.T. thinks the figures shaky.

"I couldn't tell that from your so-called presentation, Mary.

And nor unfortunately could Basil Barratt. So you see now that when I found you had slipped off home I felt it necessary to do a little investigation? I had to reassure our client, and myself, incidentally, that his account was in the right hands."

"And is it?" said Mary, bluntly. "What did you tell him when you'd been through the campaign and the copy? Did you tell him you'd fire me?"

I may as well get it over, she thought. You could play fencing games with C.D. all night, but you would not avoid the guillotine, if that was what he wanted.

He swivelled his chair half round to the window, and gazed at the pigeons again as if they might have changed since he last saw them. Mary waited in silence, watching him tap his teeth with the gold propelling pencil. They were perfect teeth, so white, so even. She wondered irrelevantly if they were his own.

"No," he said at last. "No. I didn't say I'd fire you. I told him that I had given him the best person I could find for the job and that I had every confidence in you. I asked him to trust my judgement in leaving you on the account, and that in a couple of weeks' time, that should give you time to get the overall plan finished and some idea of the television availability, we'd have another presentation. 'And she won't disappoint you this time,' I told him. 'She's got integrity and flair. She's never disappointed me.' "

He had been speaking quite gently, but now his voice changed and he jumped to his feet with an energy that sent the swivel chair whizzing.

"But will you, Mary?" he asked, walking round the desk and standing over her. "Will you disappoint us again? That's what I've been asking myself ever since I put the 'phone down on Basil Barratt. This is a big opportunity for you, you know that, but it needs all your attention and energy. Mistakes I could tolerate but, heavens girl! you seemed completely apathetic at that presentation. And look at you today; late for work and white as the beard of Father Christmas! What's the matter with you, Mary? You're not ill, are you?" And when she shook her head, he went on, "Well, whatever it is then, forget

76

about it. Boyfriend trouble? Family trouble? Sort it out away from the office. This job needs all your concentration," he jabbed a thickset finger at her, "I said *all* your concentration, if you are to make a success of it."

Looking at the pointing finger, she suddenly remembered the day that Stella had met Cecil Davies. What was it that she had said about him? That she wondered whether, if you took him out of his office, he would disappear? I must tell her I've come to the conclusion that perhaps he would, she thought. It's taken me a long time.

It had been years ago, that alarming excursion of Stella's. Mary was quite new at Markhams then, bowled over by the atmosphere of self-importance, very conscious of her need to impress everyone with her suitability for the job. Stella, who one day around noon happened to find herself in the Aldwych, suddenly felt a rare but pressing impulse to take her step-daughter out to lunch.

She had wandered in, curious and determined, and by a hideous quirk of fate had somehow ended up in C.D.'s office. Alerted by Gay of this catastrophe, Mary had roared down the passage in a torment. How *could* Stella? Surely she knew that employees' mothers did not blunder into the directors' sanctums? Heaven alone knew what impression she was producing on C.D., or in her total ignorance of the vital work he did, what appalling gaffes she was making.

But in the end I needn't have worried, thought Mary. They had that awful mock-antique cocktail cabinet open, and there they were sipping sherry. Cecil had recognised Stella from a newspaper photograph and had been flattered to receive so distinguished a guest. And Stella had been far too busy leading him on to fresh absurdities to do more than the minimum of talking. It had ended up as a pleasant memory for everyone: C.D. pleased with his brush with someone he could describe as a real artist; Stella enchanted at having met the living proof of all she had long suspected about advertising.

"So that's your famous C.D.!" she had said, more in wonder than in condemnation. "What an utterly atrocious little man!"

Poor C.D., he wasn't as bad as all that, really. Here he was giving her a second chance; being kind beyond the call of duty.

"We all think a lot of you here at Markhams," he was saying, and to her astonishment he actually patted her on the shoulder, "so pull yourself together, Mary!

"Just remember that business is business," he went on, sitting down again with the swivel chair in the interview-concluded posture, "and that, if all clients have to be handled with kid gloves, a new client is doubly sensitive. We can't afford that sort of slip up even when we've proved our worth to a customer, but when an account has just come to the agency, then it's sheer suicide."

He's right, thought Mary. He is being very decent, considering everything. Mumbling her thanks, assuring him of her whole-hearted co-operation, and trying very hard not to look like a prisoner leaving the dock on probation, she turned away and hurried from the room.

# 8

"Yes, you're almost finished," said Stella tenderly, patting the large imposing head of the eagle before her. "I wish you could see yourself."

She stood back, looking critically at the morning's work and dusting her hands on her grey overall.

"Well, what do you think, Henry?" she said aloud to the empty studio. "I wonder if you like it?"

It would have seemed almost rude, she felt, to turn away without asking his opinion; he had been so close to her while she had worked on this carving. But today it was only a rhetorical question; today she knew the bird was good.

It was Henry all right, somehow contriving to resemble him physically despite the deliberate change of form, and she knew now that she had been right to discard a straightforward approach in order to capture what had lain hidden within him. The power and intensity of the great hunched frame revealed his spirit much more readily than his own physique had ever done. In the bird could be seen all the qualities that he had managed to conceal from the world under the reticence of his manner and bearing; his staying power, his strength of purpose; the fire of his courage, of his wisdom and endurance.

Yet the set of the head and the angle of the body, that was Henry as plain as a photograph, in the most physical sense that she could show him. And the claws; there had been a certain remorseless determination about him when his mind was fixed on an objective, it had shown in his fingers, in the way he gripped things. As his prey there would have been no hope of respite. He would not have tired, or become deflected.

She touched a talon critically, remembering the strength of his long thin hands with their thong-like sinews. Yes, the essence was there.

Tears rose in her eyes and she dashed them angrily away.

How absurd I am, she thought. It's a success; I should be giving thanks, not weeping. She leaned her head against the smooth upward curve of the bird's breast, hoping to catch the elusive feeling of satisfaction, but the stone had grown comfortless. Its coldness only emphasised her lack of the real Henry, and the vivid memory of his grasp, warm and alive and responsive.

She drew back sharply. It was unreasonable to feel so rejected, and yet it was as if the bird had grown aloof and self-sufficient now that it was completed. It refused to bow to her need for consolation; that was not its business. It was a memorial, moving and perceptive as she had wished, but a memorial only. What did I expect from it, she thought dully. Did I hope to raise him, like a Lazarus, from the grave?

She straightened herself wearily and crossed to the window, looking out over the little gardens that separated the terrace from the busy roadway, to the river beyond. It was a view that seldom failed to soothe her.

This morning she saw that under the big plane tree, where the black earth had been lying empty, the tips of bulbs were appearing. They would be crocuses, she knew, purple and yellow; and then there would be daffodils, narcissus. How incredible it was to think that she would not see them flower again. It was especially difficult to accept how many things she had experienced for the last time: little things, some beautiful, some ugly, but all precious, grown valuable by repetition, woven into the fabric of over sixty years.

That she was to lose Mary, lose Robert, that this carving of Henry was the last work she would ever do, these things were so terrible, so fundamental, that she had had to turn and face them, to come to some sort of terms, however painful, with the prospect of their loss. As the weeks passed and as each day she consciously endured the thought of the parting, of the ending, she found herself a little closer to a form of resignation. In relation to the few things that mattered most to her her own death was no longer inconceivable. It was not that she minded less, but rather that she had accepted its inevitability.

But the little things were too numerous to tackle, too many-faced to comprehend. They stabbed her in the back when she was least expecting it, penetrating and savage as the blade of a dagger. Those crocuses, for instance; she had not known last year that she would not see another crocus. If she had known, she would have drunk her fill of them and then have thrust them into the dark crammed cupboard of her memory as she had forced all that paper into the hessian sack, but then she had not realised that she must make the proper goodbyes. She felt unjustly deprived, cheated of the new spring she would not live to see.

She had tried every trick to insulate herself against these moments, to make herself accept entirely her approaching death. It was terrible to find that her state of dignified resignation was skin-deep only, that it did nothing to prepare her for the truth. It was as if a part of her was beyond the reach of her reason and remained totally unprotected, refusing to wear the armour she was at such pains to forge.

She knew, for instance – she had told herself a thousand times – that this carving would be her last. She thought she had hardened herself to the bitterness of that knowledge, had lived through it and come out on the other side. Yet today, as she looked down at her hands where they busied themselves, deft and experienced, among the familiar tools, she had been pierced with anguish, as shocking and unexpected as if she was hearing the truth for the first time. She would not carve again.

She had said it so often; but now, seared by the sight of her hands, she saw that the words had conveyed nothing. She had simply been repeating phrases, parrot-fashion, to the unreceptive core of her mind. Only now did the words have any significance. Only now, looking at her hands holding the worn chisels. It was as if they sprouted from them naturally, as much part of them as the callouses on the palms, or the blunt square nails. She would not hold them again. As the truth shook her, as the finality reached her, she saw that there was no stock of anaesthetic ready for the amputation. Despite all her efforts, she was not in any way prepared.

Now she sat down heavily on the window seat with her back to the heartbreak of the budding gardens and pressed the palms of her hands against her eyes. She felt worn out by tension, as if she had spent the day picking her way across an endless mine-field where each unwary step provoked a fresh explosion.

"It's been a bad morning," she said loudly, as if to justify her weakness to an invisible observer. "A thoroughly bad morning." And she found to her surprise that she was laughing, or was she sobbing, surely not? at the banality of the words she had chosen and the matter-of-fact way in which she spoke.

You face death and oblivion, you meet darkness and extinction walking in your studio, and what do you find to say about it? 'It's been a bad morning.' That's how I express myself, thought Stella. No wonder I can't communicate with Mary. It's as if I'm acting in a farce with her, where our dialogue forces us to extremes of understatement. 'It's been a bad morning.' 'Miss Otis regrets she's unable to lunch today.'

She pressed her back against the window, subduing the choking laughter with an effort, shocked by the abyss that lay beyond the fragile life-line of her self-control. Mary. Somehow she must fix her mind on Mary. Mary was important. She must make an opportunity to talk seriously with her about Robert, about Leonie, most pressingly about herself. Her failure in that direction was no laughing matter.

I should have begun ten days ago, she thought guiltily, looking at the bird, but I had to get you finished. It had seemed vital to reserve her energy for her work in the studio. She had preserved it jealously for her carving, hoarding it up like a miser his gold against the moment she began to work, and then squandering it heedlessly, leaving herself drained and exhausted. Despite all her resolutions, she had consciously avoided being alone with Mary; she could not spare the strength for that sort of confrontation.

It had not been hard to keep out of her way. Indeed, it would have been difficult to corner her, even if she had wanted to. Mary had been constantly preoccupied, mysteriously evasive. She was never at home in the evenings, and dashed out in the mornings long before her usual time. She is avoiding me too, Stella had decided with relief. I expect she is leaving me to sort out the Leonie affair on my own. She wants to underline the fact that Robert and his disasters are my responsibility. Well, she will have to wait for a little while, that's all. I have more important things to do.

In fact, once she had decided to ignore her, Leonie proved to be remarkably little trouble. She seemed quite content to be shelved for the time being. At first she had been alarmingly apathetic, delayed shock, diagnosed Stella, with a new grim authority, but after a day or two she had roused herself and appeared to accept the change in her life with an amiable lack of interest, as if it were the most natural thing in the world. Had she seemed less placid, been less acquiescent, Stella knew she would have been forced into some kind of action. She had meant to talk with her about Robert just as soon as they all felt strong enough, but Leonie had made it so easy to postpone. She had thanked her for her offer of a temporary home as if she found such an arrangement perfectly normal, and since then she had asked no questions, given and demanded no confidences, and referred to Robert only in the most commonplace manner, as if he was a conventional son and husband who had been called away from home.

Stella was grateful for the reprieve; yet meeting her as she muddled through the house, coming upon her sitting in the most unexpected places, slumped and expressionless, staring at nothing, she was assailed by qualms of uneasiness. She could not help noticing the size and frequency of the unappetising snacks she brewed for herself in the kitchen, or the curious attitude in which she often sat, leaning forward, her arms wrapped round her own body. There was something here that she recognised, that rang a disturbing bell just outside her conscious memory. Those unfocused eyes, the obsession with food, the pronounced unkemptness of her appearance, surely she had seen all this before? She knew she should unearth the buried memory; that, however unpleasant, it would give her the insight now to deal with Leonie, but she flinched from the involvement.

Instead she dismissed the disquiet. It can wait until the carving is finished, she told herself firmly. Anyway I have given a girl a home; she's safe, well fed and cared for. I really can't be expected to do much more for her.

Now, as she stood up, she caught sight of her through the window. She looked drab and dingy in the sunlight, swamped in an old duffle coat that used to belong to Robert. Watching her bump the wheels of the carrycot clumsily down the steps, Stella was filled with irritable pity. If only Mary was at home. She could bring in some friends to cheer her up, buy her some new clothes, take her to a cinema. She must be lonely, she thought, hanging round the house all day with only a baby to talk to. She needs some company of her own age.

She sighed, remembering that this time Mary could not be counted on to support her. If there ever had been any doubt on that account, none could remain after this morning. Mary considered that Leonie was her sole responsibility, that her plight was the direct result of her indulgence of Robert. She had not put it kindly either. Stella winced, remembering the hostility in the closed face, upturned on the landing below her. 'It's about time you faced a few facts,' Mary had said, 'and stopped shutting your eyes to what's going on around you. You'll get no help from me this time; I have got my own life to lead.'

It was true, of course, and she should have expected the rebuff, but it had caught her unprepared this morning, when she had not been thinking of Leonie. For once she had been thinking only of Mary, had gone to her spontaneously and without reserve, the last two weeks forgotten in the sudden understanding that had come to her, wafting up from Henry's study, through the warped boards of her studio floor.

She had gone to work early this morning, determined to snatch some advantage from her sleeplessness, but she had found that Mary was up before her. She could hear her clearly, banging about in her office beneath her feet.

It had been Henry's room, and they had shared each other's days through the screening lath and plaster, without disturbing the illusion of privacy between them. They had made it a rule not to interrupt each other, not to question, or sympathise or offer advice, but through that floor they had grown to interpret every unconscious signal; the thump of the reference book as it landed on the desk top; the clatter of the tool flung down on the pitted table; the clearing of throats and the rasping of chair legs, they absorbed without effort the tone and significance of all such things.

Stella had often marvelled at the luck that had guided their casual selection of a room to use as Henry's study; nothing else could have brought them the same undemanding daily communion, no language have expressed so finely what could be conveyed in the rattle of each opening window, in the ring of every footfall crossing the floor. Reading the signs, they could stay in tune without striving, adjusting to the slack and taut in each other without the need for words.

She had never grown used to the silence below her. Each day she was aware of it, bleak and immutable beneath her feet, a yawning void. She had given the room to Mary, trying to draw a little comfort from the knowledge that Henry would have been pleased to have her use it, but Mary seldom worked there, and never during the day.

This morning, limp from her nightly struggle, she had been shaken by the sounds of life underneath her, hardly aware whether it was Henry or Mary she heard, but jarred by the urgent vibrations from the footsteps below. Confused by weakness and memories, she listened unhappily, unable to clear her mind for working. Drawers were wrenched open, slammed shut; something was dropped that caused a momentary silence and then a fresh outburst of commotion. What could be the matter with Henry? She had never heard him so tense and angry. But of course it wasn't Henry. Not any more. It was Mary crashing round in the study, and she was in distress by the sound of it, giving vent to her emotions because she thought she was alone. I'd never know she felt like this if she was standing beside me, thought Stella sadly. Perhaps I need this floor to sharpen my vision, like other people need spectacles.

A tiny sound was rising through the plaster, irritable and monotonous. She was tapping on the desk with a pencil maybe, or drumming on the arm of the chair with her fingers? Henry used to do that when things were not going well for him, when he was frustrated or at a loss for words.

Poor little Mary. She had seen so little of her lately, and now something had happened to upset her. Perhaps she could help her, or at least offer comfort and reassurance. She must catch her before she went out to that boring office and see what she could do.

Filled with tenderness and affection she went unsteadily out of the room and leaned over the bannisters.

"Mary!" she called softly, almost as if she might wake the cold reserved Stella who was unexpectedly sleeping, "Mary! What's the matter? Come up and see me for a minute?"

No reply. She tried again, a little louder. It was difficult to sound gentle when you had to shout to make yourself heard, but she felt so light and giddy. She could not face those stairs.

"Mary!" she cried. "Can't you hear me, Mary? I want to talk to you!"

There was a crash and a slam and there was Mary on the landing below her. She had her coat on, and a woolly hat that made her look absurdly young. Stella could almost see the bulky plaits sticking out beneath it, bouncy and nearly horizontal, as they had done when she was a child.

"What's the matter, Stella?" she said abruptly, crossly. "Why are you up so early? I can't stop now; I'm already late for the office."

"But it's only eight o'clock," said Stella, stung by the unreasonable haste, and by the impatient tone in which the words were spoken. "Surely you don't have to go yet? It only takes you fifteen minutes."

"We're very busy just now," said Mary with a calculated calm that irked her. She sounded like those nurses at the hospital, as if she was explaining the obvious to an idiot.

"I don't expect you have noticed," she went on, "but I have been leaving early for nearly a fortnight. I have a demanding job and there are times when I cannot let Robert or anyone else distract me. I have my own life to lead, however pointless it may seem to you."

"I'm sorry to have delayed you," said Stella. She really was sorry, if Mary was in such a hurry, but she was aware that she probably sounded sarcastic, as though she put no weight on the importance of her job. "I thought you sounded upset about something. I didn't want to discuss Robert, or Leonie either, for that matter . . ."

"As for Leonie," interrupted Mary, homing in on the name as if it was the excuse she wanted to attack her, "Leonie is your problem. Leonie would not be here if you had brought up Robert properly. It's about time you faced a few facts about this son of yours, and stopped shutting your eyes to what's going on around you. You'll get no help from me this time." She paused and repeated belligerently, as though anticipating contradiction, "I've just told you – I have my own life to lead."

Looking at the shuttered face, Stella knew that she had misjudged her moment. There would be no breaking through to Mary this morning; everything she said would be taken up wrongly.

"All right," she said wearily. "Don't think I misunderstand you. Off you go if you have business to attend to. I'll deal with my problems perfectly well without you. In my own way. In my own time."

My own time, she thought. There isn't much, can't you see it? Time is a commodity you are rich in, Mary, but there isn't much left for me.

Watching Mary's face, she saw the shadow cross it, a doubt, a wavering, a fleeting crack in her determination.

"Go on," she said, nervous that she had appealed for comfort where she had wished to give it. "Go on and get to your office early, if that's what you need to do this morning. I'll see you later, when you're not in such a hurry."

Mary had hesitated, rubbing the back of one leg with the other foot as she always did in moments of stress.

"I really am busy," she said suddenly, as if Stella doubted her truthfulness. "I've a presentation coming up that means a great deal to me. I expect it's making me edgy, but there's not long to go."

She bent and picked up her bag and a huge quantity of files from the bottom of the staircase.

"You'll be all right, won't you?" she added unexpectedly,

still looking down at the armful of paper. "I want to have a talk with you too, when this rush is over. You are looking very tired. Perhaps you should have a holiday?"

"Oh, I'm all right," said Stella hastily, stepping back into the shadow of the curtain. "You run along and show C.D. the stuff you're made of. You know how I would hate to keep him waiting."

And Mary had gone, banging the heavy door behind her, while she had turned back to the emptiness of her studio, and to her carving which seemed the only thing she was adequately fitted to do.

"But you are only stone," she said now to the eagle. "Mary has far more of Henry in her. You are less than Mary. Less than the part of Henry that lives on in her. I cannot reach the Henry in Mary, and so I create you of my insufficiency. But you are only a lump of stone."

She turned to the bird with her hand extended as though asking it to contradict her, and noticed for the first time that beyond it the door of the studio was swinging open and that a man was standing silently behind the carving, along the line of her outflung arm.

# 9

Robert! she thought, in the split second before her eyes focused properly. But the next instant she saw that he was not at all like Robert. He was much taller for a start, and heavier; a big gangling good-looking young man in a city suit that seemed to be too small for him. She was sure she had seen him somewhere before. Where could it have been? I used to have a flair for remembering faces, she thought despairingly, and now that's going too.

"I'm sorry to have startled you," he was saying apologetically. "I knocked several times but I thought you didn't hear me, so I am afraid I just came in."

A beautiful voice. Yes, of course, now she remembered. He was that friend of Mary's who had come to see her when she was ill. He had been so charming and had called so often. How could she have forgotten such a thing?

"How nice to see you," she began.

She became aware suddenly that her arm was still thrown out in a gesture of supplication and dropped it hurriedly, remembering with exasperation that she had been speaking aloud to her carving. Had he been there all the time, too polite to interrupt her? How very embarrassing; she hoped he did not think she had gone mad.

"Have you been there long?" she enquired anxiously. "I'm sorry I didn't hear you. When I get wrapped up in my work I'm deaf to interruptions."

"No . . . no," he said vaguely, as if it was of no consequence.

She searched his face for signs of pity or amusement, but he was looking intently at the eagle. Perhaps he had not heard her, or at least not taken in what she was saying. One must hope for the best.

"Mary must be very like her father," he said thoughtfully,

indicating the bird. "Perhaps it's the attitude that is so typical, but I would know at once that she was a relation."

He put an exploratory hand on the eagle's head, as if trying to get to know it better, and curiously Stella felt no resentment. She usually had a physical dislike of people touching her carvings, especially when they were newly born.

"Yes, there was a great resemblance," she said, pleased that this nice young man had found a likeness to Henry in Mary. "They were very alike too in temperament and disposition. Both proud and reserved. And loyal." She paused, looking at the large hand resting so confidently on the bird's stony feathers, suddenly recalling his name and the tone in which Mary spoke of him.

"Not people one should take lightly, Barrie," she added sharply. "Not people one should play around with."

He smiled at once with a winning ease that made her heart sink and yet warmed her despite herself. She could see what Mary found to charm her in this agreeable bear-like creature. He radiated an attraction that she recognised even at her age, and in her condition. I had it too, she thought, and it wasn't easy to live with. I kept thinking that people were interested in me as a person, and then found that they only desired me as a sexual partner. Perhaps that's why I took so long to commit myself to Henry; I had stopped expecting such things to last.

"I wouldn't have come to see you today," he was saying, "to tell you I was playing around. I don't take Mary lightly."

"I'm glad," she said sincerely, surprised to find how easily she believed him. "Life is not easy for Mary at the moment, and I would not like to think," she paused, meeting his eyes for the first time and startled by the shrewdness of their expression, "I would not like to think that she was completely unsupported?"

She knew she had framed the remark as a question, and was annoyed to find that she appeared to be turning the conversation into an interview. She might as well have asked him if his intentions were completely honourable, and that did not do these days. Still, he seemed encouraged rather than disconcerted.

"I'm very concerned about Mary," he said earnestly. "I'm

all set to be supportive. I have known her a long time, and I'd have hoped that she might feel inclined to share her problems with me. But she doesn't," he went on. "She seems to have no intention of letting me help her, and I'm worried about her, that's the truth of it. I suppose that's why I came to see you – to find out whether you could throw some light on what's troubling her?"

He came round the bird, and perched with unceremonious grace on the edge of the dusty table.

"Oh, I know she has some bother at the office," he went on, "and that she is upset about her brother and his girlfriend. But I don't see why that should make her try to avoid me. It's more than the job, or Robert. It's as if she had lost confidence in herself as a person."

He glanced up at her, abruptly himself the inquisitor. "I thought you might know why," he said. "She's so very fond of you, and from one or two things she has indicated, I have rather gathered. . ."

He stopped, perhaps seeing the alarm in her face, and shrugged hopelessly.

"But of course, if you would rather not talk about it I can only apologise. I wouldn't have come except that I know she needs help and I no longer seem able to give it. I know she was very upset when her father died, and things like that do come back at you when you are disturbed, but. . ."

His voice trailed off.

"But what?" said Stella impatiently.

"Well," he said slowly. He sounded uncomfortable. "Well, she seemed to be worried about you."

"Did she say so?"

"Not exactly. She doesn't share her problems easily. I've just told you that."

He wandered over to the window and Stella waited while he picked absently at a blister on the chipping paintwork.

"She has nightmares," he said abruptly. "She talks in her sleep. It makes me feel like a spy sometimes, and yet I listen. It's the only way I can know what's going on beneath the shell she concocts around her."

He turned to Stella, his hand flung out in much the same gesture as she had just used towards the eagle.

"Why doesn't she trust me?" he said. "Why can't she confide in me? Did she find me nothing more than a passing source of amusement? I suppose so."

He turned away, dropping his hand, and resumed his destructive work on the blister. "I'm not blaming Mary," he went on. "It's not the first time this has happened. I don't seem capable of sustaining an intimate relationship or inspiring any lasting affection. Once the novelty has worn off I become redundant. My wife certainly found me so."

"Your wife?"

"My wife left me," he said flatly. "Oh . . . several years ago. I hardly ever see her these days. As far as my relationship with Mary is concerned she simply doesn't come into the picture."

"Indeed," said Stella, without conviction.

At least he's a bad liar, she thought. An unhappy liar; more anxious, perhaps, to convince himself than to mislead me. She had a sudden vivid picture of Robert, who lied so expertly, so adroitly; who could throw her on the instant into a confusion of hope and doubt, the old sour churn where the desire to believe him curdled unpleasantly with the reluctance to be duped again.

But this was no Robert. When Barrie said he valued Mary, it was clear that he was speaking the truth; when he said the existence of his wife counted for nothing, he was obviously lying. He was not devious; rather he was affectionate and troubled and he had said some worrying things about Mary. She must concentrate on him and obliterate the image of Robert and the perverse longing it had aroused in her to be with him, despite the lies, despite the failures. Her son. If she closed her eyes she could see him so clearly, dazzling among the carvings, the only living thing she had ever made. She needed his warmth, his vigour, the promise he carried of life continued.

But she must not lose herself like this; not now, when she was needed. It would not do. She blinked furiously to dispel the vision, and found that Barrie was now beside her; indeed that he seemed to be supporting her, was actually holding her arm.

"I'm sorry," she said, furious at allowing such a lapse, and attempting to sound as casual as possible. "I get giddy when I stand too long. I always have. I should have sat down ages ago – I've been working all morning."

"I know just how it is." He took his cue politely. If she did not want a fuss he was not going to make one. "I often get the same sensation. The blood seems to drain from your head."

He helped her to a chair and propped himself up against the rungs of the open step-ladder beside her. She smiled at him, pleased to find him so real again and aware of a feeling of comradeship that seemed to be rooted deeper than in their common concern for Mary.

What had he said that had touched such a chord of memory? 'Once the novelty has worn off I become redundant.' She recognised that feeling, had experienced it herself, before Henry, a score of times. But she had come early to terms with the power of her own sexuality, had accepted that she possessed a rare degree of physical magnetism that had nothing to do with her personality. I was lucky, she thought. Perhaps it is always lucky to be selfish. I enjoyed the power and I escaped the bitterness. I gave too little to such relationships to feel rejected when the time came for parting.

But that was long ago. She must fix her mind on the actual, on the present. Barrie was not selfish, and it had not necessarily been to his advantage that, to use one of Robert's odious phrases, he turned women on. She could see that brief easy conquests would not be much good if you were looking for warmth, understanding, affection. You would awake desire indiscriminately and then mistake it for something deeper; it would be tempting to conclude that you had nothing more valuable to offer, when so few of those who wanted you were looking for anything more.

"But Mary is not like that," she said, following her train of thought and forgetting that for him the remark might have no relevance. "I cannot see Mary involve herself in anything so superficial."

"As me?" he said. "Well, that certainly is a blunt assessment."

It should have been a joke, she could see that he did not believe that this had been her meaning, but it was said too sharply to be funny, and looking up at his face she saw he had not smiled.

He would make an interesting portrait, she thought. The unconscious appeal, the clumsiness that somehow enhanced it, the bitter lines around the mouth that spoke more of the person within than did the open smile that belied them; yes, it would not be easy. Maybe Robert, with his alarming ability to peel back façades, could capture him better.

"What are you thinking?"

He spoke gently, hardly breaking the drift of her reverie, and she heard his words absently, regretting that his voice should be such a distinctive part of him, since it would not be possible to reproduce it on canvas.

"I was wondering how Robert would paint you," she said frankly. "You've the sort of face that interests him. He'd say it needed decoding; he is very good at that."

"Robert! God forbid! I'll go to a surgeon, thank you, when I want to be dismembered." He grinned suddenly. "Do you know Daphne Creighton, by any chance?"

Stella nodded.

"Well, so do I – and much better too, now that Robert has finished painting her. He should have *been* a surgeon, now I come to think of it. It's a knife he uses, not a paintbrush."

"Yes, poor Daphne," said Stella insincerely. "And she gave a party for it!"

They laughed together, guiltily, like conspirators. I like you, thought Stella. I suppose I should think of you as a stranger, but you've always felt like a friend.

"He has painted Mary," she added. "Often. But he has never reached the core of her. I think he is ashamed, or jealous. Both, perhaps, but anyway he baulks at doing her justice."

"Yes . . . Mary," the laughter had died out of his face. "We none of us are very good at getting to the core of Mary, are we? And yet I think that's what she needs. She's so defensive, almost as if she is starved of something, of appreciation, perhaps, but maybe she could not accept that from someone", he glanced half mockingly at Stella, "as superficial as me."

"Don't fence with me Barrie," she said. "I don't feel strong enough for games. I meant – and you know it – that she doesn't care to involve herself in shallow relationships. But she is proud and she's afraid of rejection, of exposing herself to failure. She has had enough of that from Robert; from me too, perhaps, though I've tried, I *thought* I'd tried, to reassure her. She is insecure, if you like. She needs some gesture, some evidence of faith to give her confidence."

She hesitated, gazing down at her worn hands, skilled only in the fashioning of stone, wishing they could remould the living.

"I love her," she said at last, "but I cannot convey it. Long ago, perhaps . . . if I had tried harder. But now it is too late. What can I say that would change the impressions of a lifetime?"

She looked up at her carving, more as if she were appealing to the bird than to Barrie.

"So many years," she went on. "Always so much between us. Robert, her father, my work, pushing her onto the sidelines, making her fight to establish an identity. In the end we all became her sparring partners. This ridiculous job she does, she only took it to defy us, to underline the fact that she had independent interests. I didn't take it seriously. I poked fun at it; tore it to ribbons. I thought it was a phase, a passing rebellion against our values. Perhaps it was. But it lasted, and now it has become another wedge between us."

She paused, but Barrie remained silent.

"We abrade each other. It is almost like a compulsion. As though we were driven to belittle each other, to criticise, to compete. It has been like that from the beginning. She would not believe me now if I were to tell her that I trust and admire her, and I could find no words to express it. It would take more than words. If I could give her something of myself – something that would show her."

She stopped. Something that would show her. The bird, she

thought. I will give her the carving. It will not be a memorial, but a private offering, a bond between myself and Mary. It will live, it will show her the love that refuses other expression. Even if she does not feel for it, surely she will understand what it signified to me? She will know that it is a gift of the effort, of the vision; of everything that has made my life worth while.

She looked up, and her joy died. Seeing the shock on his face, forgetting that she had not spoken aloud, she misread the cause of his distress.

"Why do you look at me like that?" she cried. "It is all I have to give her. I have so little time."

"You are ill," he said.

She felt limp with relief. It was only concern for her that made him look so grave; he had not rejected the offering of the carving.

"I am dying," she said simply.

Immediately, guiltily, she was astonished at how easily the taboo had been broken. For there was a taboo, a prohibition against the mention of death in that particular context that had often amazed her, but that she had conscientiously observed. Until you were *in extremis* – and even then you were pushing good manners to their farthest limits – you did not admit you would not recover. You could say you were ill, and if necessary add in a hushed voice that the illness was a grave one, like heart disease or cancer; but you must not point out to people that you were dying.

In healthy society you do not use, and do not hear, those words. By unwritten agreement they are banned from the vocabulary. It is tacitly understood that no person of good taste would employ them. Other cumbersome phrases are dragged in. You can receive a 'poor prognosis', or things can 'be going rather badly'. You can have a 'disappointing reaction' to a treatment that everyone knows is vital. Later, you can even be described as 'growing weaker' (which allows for the fatuous reply that tomorrow you may turn the corner), but whatever you say you must give your listener the chance to escape the embarrassment of your dilemma, to pretend to believe the disaster can be averted. It is outrageous to reply to a conventional enquiry that you are dying.

Well, now she had said so; had committed the ultimate breach of etiquette, and she had to admit that she felt much better for it. She even felt a pleasing curiosity as to how this polite young man would react to such an uncivilised statement. He could hardly reply that he hoped she would soon feel better.

"I am dying," she said again, determined not to go back on a course that relieved her of so many idiotic platitudes. It would not do if he pretended not to hear her.

There was a pause.

"I see," said Barrie slowly. He left the ladder and squatted in the dust beside her, his hand on the arm of her chair. "I see. I am very sorry."

Touched by his acceptance, she put her hand over his, and they sat for a moment without speaking.

"You have not told Mary," he said at last. It was more of a statement than a question.

She shook her head. "I'm trying to."

"Would you like me to tell her?" he said gently, and seeing that look on her face he went on at once, "No. No, I can see that would not be the answer. She would feel you had betrayed the affection between you. She must be the first to know.

"But she senses it in a way," he went on. "She knows that you are hiding something from her. She feels shut out, excluded. She is worried and hurt too, because she thinks that if she mattered to you, you would confide in her.

"I know," he continued, acknowledging her attempt to interrupt him, "I know it is not like that. You don't need to tell me. But that's how it seems to her."

"Will you help her?"

"I don't know if she wants me, you must remember that. But if she will let me . . . yes, I will try to help her. Perhaps if she knew how much you loved her she would see . . . she would see."

"That you also love her?"

"Yes. But she may not be much comforted by that."

He sat back on his heels and brushed his trousers with an

97

angry automatic action, as if he had said more than he intended and wanted to wipe away the words.

"But you," he went on. "Can't I be of some use to you? Can't I help you? Is there nothing that can be done about . . . about your illness?"

The dust eddied round them and Stella caught her breath sharply. She must not begin to cough. Not now. The cough was a hurdle of the early morning, and she paid it a price that rose steeply according to the amount of rest she had enjoyed. She had begun to see it as a live thing, possessed of a conscious malice, in league with the tumour that provoked it. After a good night it would fall on her with increased fury, as if determined to destroy her efforts to refresh herself.

It won't obey me any longer, she thought wildly. I cannot control it. It was as though a cringing servant, once barely acknowledged and thanklessly used, had abruptly seized power. Now that the tables were turned the cough used her spitefully, exulting in her degradation. Wait till I'm alone, she besought it. You can do what you like then, you have won anyway. Only be generous and spare me now.

"I have cancer," she said aloud, fixing her eyes on the solid kneeling figure beside her.

She must hold her concentration. They were frightening, these lapses. More and more often she found herself talking like this, arguing, cajoling, reproving her body as if it had an independent existence. Conversing with her disease like a madwoman. . . But she was not mad. Barrie must not think her mad.

"I am being treated for it," she went on, trying to inhale carefully, steadily. "I am in the hands of . . . of a most competent specialist."

She paused as Dr. Zuckerman loomed before her, inhuman and dispassionate, coolly dispensing life and death. Self-assured. Detestable. I should visit him tomorrow, she thought, recoiling from the prospect, and this time, whatever I do, he will see. . .

"Yes. A most competent specialist," she repeated firmly. "But I don't think there is much more he can do. The treatment

98

is very – severe. I have had all I can take of it. And my chest. . .''

She shut her eyes. She must collect herself. She could not inflict Barrie with details of her illness, of her decay and her terror.

"No," she went on. "Nothing would help me more than to feel that there was someone left to love, to look after Mary."

She opened her eyes, her gaze straying past him, fixing on the shaft of sun that slanted through the window. It looked solid as a pillar, shimmering with particles of powdered stone. It was pointed towards her – a huge lance held by an invisible giant; but it was beautiful.

"Try and trust her," she said, measuring the precious breath. "Mary does not tire of people. She is like her father – a builder, not a destroyer."

She stopped. It was useless. The impulse to cough was strangling her. Soon she would be prostrated, debased to the level where nothing existed but the achievement of the next breath.

She must make him leave. It was suddenly the only thing that mattered – that she should not be seen in this disgusting secret extremity.

She lifted her hands as if to thrust him from her.

"Away," she gasped. "Go away."

Who was he, anyway? He had ceased to exist as a person; he had become nothing more than a threat to her privacy. She had forgotten that he was Barrie; had forgotten about Mary; and the words she had wanted to say to him had faded, blotted out by the overpowering need to be alone.

She glared at him, trapped like an animal by her impotence, desiring only to hide herself, but without the strength to run away.

But the panic and the fear of humiliation lasted only a moment before she felt the cough seize her; drowning all feeling, sucking her into a whirlpool where nothing but the fight for air had any significance; horribly and yet mercifully obliterating all other thoughts from her mind.

# 10

The little Italian restaurant was crowded, but after her long absence Signor Molocco had welcomed Mary like a queen, clearing a group of young men from her favourite corner table with a ferocious spate of Italian, and beaming her into a chair. It was a cheerful, noisy place, always a cherished haunt of Robert's, and she was glad to be back. She liked the fat proprietor and his smiling wife, and recognised with pleasure the usual hoard of cousins, aunts and grandmothers, and the profusion of useful good-looking children. She could hear them now, crashing round the kitchen, banging pots and pans and shouting to each other. Somebody, perhaps Signor Molocco himself? was singing in an ebullient tenor voice.

It seemed to Mary that they only opened at lunchtime for company and conversation. Nearly all the customers were Italian, and most of them appeared to be friends or relations of the Moloccos. She supposed that there must be some sort of family agreement, for she seldom saw them pay. They came and went in droves, crying out greetings and farewells, and dragging the chairs and tables about at will to increase the capacity of the seating arrangements.

In the evenings it was all quite different. Signora Molocco's food was good, and had gained quite a reputation. It was often difficult to get a table, but the Italian clientele vanished, or were swept behind the service hatch. It always amused Mary to see the transformation; the room candlelit and decorous; Signor Molocco, glorious in a dinner jacket, his hair slicked back with oil, his singing silenced, and the rest of his family concealed behind the firmly shut kitchen doors.

Candlelight was kind to the decor, to the smoky paint and the rickety furniture. It hid the dust on the floor and the spots on the not-quite-clean checked tablecloths. It obscured the place where the youngest Molocco had picked the wallpaper off the wall. The English customers did not slam the door or move the chairs around. They did not shout, or laugh immoderately, and remained seated where Signor Molocco placed them. It was all very elegant and restrained – and much more expensive. Mary could see that the Moloccos were inordinately proud of the image they had created.

For herself, she preferred it as it was now, down-at-heel and grubby in the sunlight, with Signor Molocco in his shirt sleeves, at once more foreign and more genial, embracing his relatives and sitting down at the tables; opening large raw-looking carafes of wine that were not to be seen later on in the day.

It was difficult, sitting here, to remember that Robert was a monster; to revive the horror and repugnance she had felt for him on the barge. She had tried to be late, hoping to avoid the softening effects of the familiar setting and Signor Molocco's welcome, but the tedious bus journey and uncomfortable loitering had been so much wasted effort; however late you contrived to be, Robert always managed to be later still.

Mary sighed, picking a blob of candle-wax off the used tablecloth. She was a fool to have bothered. It was a family institution, this waiting for Robert; in the time-table of every expedition she could remember since her girlhood, a standard period of grace had to be added to allow for Robert's inevitable unpunctuality. 'Let's meet at seven,' Stella would say, cheerfully cutting her own day short in the face of such obvious necessity. 'That should allow us plenty of time to wait for Robert.' And they would bustle and hurry in order to arrive at the appointed moment, because, in some mysterious fashion, they knew that if they were late, then Robert would be proportionately later still. It was as if he had a sixth sense that alerted him the instant that they began their vigil. He could always keep them waiting no matter how dilatory their own time-keeping happened to be.

Today it had almost been a relief to find that the pattern had not altered. It would have seemed unnatural to have found Robert sitting at the table, as if the whole fabric of their lives had suffered a frightening sea-change and that nothing would ever be the same again.

But of course nothing could be the same again. Had it not been for the intervention of luck, Robert would have killed, murdered, Toby. The preposterous fact must be faced and somehow prevented from recurring. She had tried so hard not to think about it during these last few days; she could not afford her own rage and disgust to blurr her concentration on the work that was vital to her success at Markhams. After all, Leonie was secure, for the moment, in her own house. Dealing with Robert would have to wait. Deep down too, she acknowledged that if brought face to face with Robert she might not be able to lie about her own involvement in Leonie's disappearance. She certainly did not want him, vicious and aggressive, intruding in a situation that was already difficult enough to cope with. Later, when Leonie and the baby were well, and could go elsewhere, undiscovered and in safety. But for the time being she did not trust herself to make contact. It had not occurred to her that Robert might wish to see her, that he would be the one to get in touch.

She had been taken off guard when she heard his voice on the telephone – his light diffident family voice, so disarmingly like their father's – and she had discovered that she had agreed to meet him. Had agreed, in fact, with abject enthusiasm, eager to see him, to disprove, perhaps, what she knew perfectly well to be true. Well, she thought defensively, maybe I can use the opportunity to confess how worried I am about Stella; maybe I can enlist his help without involving Leonie. Perhaps he would not be drunk at lunchtime; perhaps he would be sympathetic, supportive, invigorating as only Robert could be. She should have been angry and vindictive, but here she was, useless to deny it, as hungry for his presence as she had been in dread of it at Chiswick, only a few days ago.

At least I am prepared, she thought, and if he has been drinking I will say as little as I can, and leave him.

She lifted her eyes and there he was, painfully vivid and familiar, springing in from the street with his agile cat-like tread.

"Mary!" he said. "You're here before me! And I thought I had timed it perfectly." He looked at his watch with an expression of exquisite horror. "Why, it's half-past one! How can it be? It's disgraceful, I'm late again! And now I expect you're furious?"

He met her eye and laughed.

"No, honestly," he said, dropping the affectation, "I did try this time. I'm sorry."

He came round the table and kissed her, his arm on the back of her chair.

No smell of drink, she thought with relief, and he looks quite sober. Not flushed or glassy-eyed. Not even a hangover.

"Well, isn't that a relief?" he said, sitting down opposite her and putting his elbows on the table.

"Isn't what a relief?" she asked as crossly as she could manage. Really, it was hopeless. Why did she feel so pleased to see him?

"That I don't smell of drink!" he said at once, with a grin that was half spiteful, half affectionate. "That on this occasion at least I am plainly stone cold sober."

Mary felt herself flushing.

"I don't know what you mean. . ." she began, but he interrupted her cheerfully.

"Oh, come off it Mab! You've always been an open book, and you may as well admit it. Sniff, sniff, you went," he threw back his head, assuming a strained, anxious expression. "Sniff, sniff, *sniff*. Why, how astonishing! What a miracle! Not a trace, not a whiff, of the dreaded odour!"

He relapsed in his chair with an exaggerated show of satisfaction. "It certainly is surprising – but goodness, *such* a relief!

"You're becoming unbearably pompous," he went on, in his own voice. "And stuffy. And censorious. You make me wish I had arrived absolutely pickled, but there it is, I haven't. Another time, perhaps."

"I'll look forward to that," said Mary dryly, but she laughed nonetheless. He was a good mimic and she felt like laughing anyway – because it was, as he said, such a relief.

"That's better," he said. "You are not really pompous, are

you Mary? It's just that you are Jekyll and I'm Hyde – two parts of a far from perfect whole. I always forget that when you are not with me."

"It must be awful," he added, "suddenly seeing me before you. Specially when I'm drunk. Like meeting yourself in a distorting mirror." He sighed. "No wonder you would like to reform me."

He sat up with a bound, and jerked his chair in to the table.

"Anyway," he went on, "since reform's unnecessary today, let's make the bickering wait and enjoy ourselves for a little. We don't need these things . . ." he took the menu from her hand and put it with his on the next table, "there's nothing edible on them, not till the evening. We always have lasagne here at lunchtime. Don't you remember? Lasagne and salad."

"Yes," she said. "Of course we do. Lasagne and salad."

He filled her glass and she sipped it wonderingly. "This wine," she went on, "I wonder where he gets it? It's unique all right. It tastes as if he had it shipped straight from his own village."

"Where alas, they are abysmally unskilled at wine making."

"But blessed in their relationship with Signor Molocco. . . Oh no, Robert! It just misses being disgusting. When you get used to it, it's really rather delightful."

"Unlike me?" said Robert edgily, and she glanced up in dismay, not liking the tone, or the springy poised way he sat.

"Yes, it's the other way round with me, isn't it Mary? At first you might be excused for thinking me almost delightful; but as you get used to me you realise that I am really rather disgusting!"

He's not joking, she thought. And after all, that's just what I do find myself thinking. She looked at him, almost hoping to glimpse the violence, the cruelty, the monster that she had pictured so constantly in his absence; but all she saw was her brother, whom she loved, now sitting silent before her.

"Robert!" she said weakly, unwilling to take up the cudgel now that he had handed it to her so neatly. "It was you who suggested that we should enjoy ourselves. Don't let's quarrel!"

"Haven't we come here to quarrel?" He looked at her,

raising his eyebrows, and she dropped her gaze miserably to the table.

"Well, all right," he went on. "Let's eat first, if you like. And quarrel later. Better for the digestion, as Mother would say. How is she, by the way? I haven't seen her for, oh, weeks now."

He picked up his fork and began to eat ravenously.

"Come on, then," he said between mouthfuls, "tell me about Mother! I really want to know, and surely that should provide a safe topic of conversation?"

Mary took up her glass and resolutely drained it. After all, this was what she had wanted to talk about. It was absurd to think that today they could have been happy together. Today, or any day.

"There are not many safe topics left," she said slowly. "They seem to be a dying breed, don't they? In fact, Stella was one of the things I wanted to discuss with you. I'm very worried about her. I don't think she is well."

Robert did not look up, but he stopped eating, his fork poised halfway to his mouth.

"Do you want to leave her till after lunch, then?" he said. "It seems a pity to ruin such very good lasagne?"

"No!" said Mary loudly.

She could see Stella's face above her on the landing. Greyish, it had been, drawn and unslept. She had thought it was a trick of the light – a shadow cast by the curtain. But it hadn't been. Speaking the words to Robert made it suddenly quite clear that it hadn't been.

"I tell you, she's ill," she went on urgently. "And I don't mean she is getting a cold or influenza. I'm afraid that there's something really the matter with her, and I want . . . I want you to find out what it is, Robert. I'd never get it out of her, she would clam up like an oyster. I don't even know how to begin."

She had his attention now, and she ploughed on desperately, determined to involve him and yet alarmed at how convincing she sounded, at how well the pieces of jig-saw fitted together.

She told him of the distressing contents of Stella's bathroom cabinet, of the bottles and pills so numerous that there was actually a chart to help her keep track of them; she described Stella's thinness, her pallor, her obsession with her slowly moving carving. She found herself speaking of all sorts of things she had not consciously known she had noticed; of Stella's increasing vagueness, of how seldom she appeared at mealtimes and how little she ate when she did so; of how she occasionally met her, standing listless on the half-landings, almost as if she was afraid to climb the stairs.

She was about to embark on Stella's extraordinary manner the night that Leonie had arrived when she remembered that this was forbidden territory and that the sympathetic face in front of her was in fact the same untrustworthy vicious Robert whom Stella had so strangely defended.

The words died in her throat, and the release that she had felt in confiding in Robert died painfully with them. How could she trust him, lean on him, ask for his help when so much treacherous ground was lying rank between them? There was no Robert. Nothing but an empty mask that offered false understanding, false affection. It was horrible. Appallingly – and yet why worry about Robert, himself so shameless? She felt her eyes fill with tears.

Robert jumped up, pushing aside the clutter of plates between them. She felt him thrust something into her hands; an enormous handkerchief, or was it a piece of rag, covered with paint and charcoal. She buried her face in it and was engulfed in the smell of tobacco and turpentine – the distinctive age-old smell of the comforting Robert, of the Robert who was so easily moved to staunch tears he had not caused; and yet, in other moods, so ruthlessly provoked them.

But she reached for his hand, swept back by the smell to other crises, other handkerchiefs. How could he be so compassionate and yet so cruel? For he was compassionate sometimes, touchingly moved and concerned by other peoples' misery. By her misery. Unless, as so often, he was the source of it.

"Mab!" he was saying now. "Don't cry, Mab. I can't bear it when you cry!"

He leaned over the table, spilling a wine glass as he did so, and patted her soothingly on the shoulder. A plate fell to the floor and someone scurried forward to scrape up the mess; faces were turned eagerly towards them.

With anyone else she would have been embarrassed; she could not, would not have let herself behave like this. But with Robert it was different. As far as Robert was concerned, she knew the room might as well have been empty. Shocked looks, staring crowds, outraged codes of behaviour – they simply passed him by. It was not that he flouted them, he simply did not notice that they existed. Once enlisted he was all yours, single-minded and unselfconscious.

It was his great strength; it went far to cancel out the score she held against him. He had been so hurtful in the home, goading, mocking, sowing distrust between herself and Stella. He had taunted her triumphantly, stirring up mischief even in her sound relationship with Father. And yet outside, in the barbaric bewildering world of communal childhood, he had been her champion; younger only in years, older always in confidence.

Dreadful childhood. Trackless adolescence. She remembered so well the hurts, the quarrels, the cold-shouldering; she dreamt of them still – the fights and falls, the insults, the real and imagined failures. And Robert . . . Robert, who was not constrained by any urge to fit the conventional mould of boyhood; who did not mind looking a fool; who made and dropped friends without regard for their opinion. He had sought her out in the maelstrom – at parties, on picnics, in playgrounds – when he noticed that things were bad. "Cheer up, Mab! Cheer up!" Coming to her where she stood alone, scuffing the gravel with her toe, holding back the tears "Don't cry, Mab! Don't cry!" Other boys would have pretended not to see her, have hurried by. It was disconcerting enough to have anything so silly as a sister, without having one who cried. But Robert had not cared what other boys thought. He did not care now.

Perhaps that's what is wrong with you, she thought. You are not bound by ordinary strictures, conventional censures. You can respond to an audience, goodness knows. No one can play to the gallery more cunningly, more merrily than you. But when the moment passes, the audience is dead for you. They have served their turn; it does not matter what they think any longer. You do not feel responsible to anyone, except yourself, and whatever passion happens to consume you.

"Maybe it's not so bad as you think," he was saying. "We'll sort it out, don't you worry. We'll find out what is wrong with her and put it right between us. Cheer up, Mab. Be a brave girl."

She looked at him blearily, blowing her nose on the grimy rag that brought so much solace.

"Will you ask her about the bottles?" she asked anxiously. Somehow it was the worst thing – all that medicine. Weird and ominous and unexplained.

"Of course I will. Though I can't imagine why you haven't asked her yourself, long ago."

She shook her head hopelessly. "I couldn't. . . How will you say you found it, anyway?"

"Oh, Mab! You're an idiot. I'll go to see her, of course. Then off to the lavatory, 'Must just have a pee, Mother.' I'll open the bathroom cabinet, that's where you said she kept them, wasn't it – and out they'll all come.

" 'Mother!' I'll shout. 'What on earth is all this stuff for? What's this awful chart about? Are you turning into a health crank?' And she'll tell me, or I will prise it out of her. Simple. . ."

He flung his hands up in the air. "I can't see what's the bother."

Mary looked at him in wonder.

"But how will you explain opening her bathroom cabinet?"

"Mab! For heaven's sake! Stella is my *mother*. Why shouldn't I open her cabinet? I'll tell her – oh, anything. That I wanted to see what mouthwash she was using."

Of course he made it sound simple. But it wouldn't have been like that if she had tried. She had often attempted to establish it, this free unstudied intimacy that Robert found so easy. But it did not work. She could not get it right. She could not begin to prise things out of Stella.

"Thank you!" she said wearily. She must not be jealous of Robert's effortless relationship with his mother. It was enough that he would find out what was wrong with her; that he was on her side.

"When will you see her?" she went on, suddenly remembering Leonie, and the unpleasant complications of a sudden visit from Robert.

"Oh, after the weekend. I'm going down to the country." He paused, looking at her knowingly, cunningly. "That should give you time to sort out all your devious arrangements."

He grinned, but his face changed. His teeth were small, very white and childish and even, but the two canines were longer than the others, sharp and pointed. They made him look predatory sometimes, underlining the feline energy of his frame. Just now, she did not like his smile.

"I would suggest," he went on, "that you might want to powder your nose. But that might be difficult, mightn't it? Under the circumstances, I mean?"

He was holding something up that caught the light and glittered. It took her a minute to realise what it was that he held so delicately in front of her, balanced tantalisingly between his wiry finger and thumb.

"I found it in Toby's cot, the night that Leonie vanished. A powder compact. It's yours, by the look of it. 'M.L.' In diamonds too – very chaste . . . very expensive. . . Funny, when you haven't been around the barge for such donkeys ages?"

"What have you done with them?" he went on witheringly. "Abducted them to a place of safety? Taken them away from the evil attentions of your drunken brother? Very altruistic of you, Mary. Very commendable."

He rocked back on his chair, looking at the powder compact, turning it over in his hand as if guessing what weight it was.

"Oh, it all fell into place," he said, "once I had found this elegant little bauble. Everything packed to perfection, much better than Leonie could have managed, poor kid, nothing broken or spilt; nothing forgotten. And two cups washed up – *washed up*, I repeat, in the midst of all that squalor – neatly put on the draining board. All the marks of Mary, once you were looking in the right direction."

"I'd have come round long ago, only I thought I'd let you have your fill of them, if that was what you wanted. And it intrigued me to see whether you would have the courage to tell me, to hear my side of the matter. I thought Mother would have taken me on . . . but then, you say she is ill, and perhaps she has other things to wrestle with."

He looked up at her, and put the compact down beside her plate, quite gently.

"I was angry," he said. "And you, for different reasons – well, you are also angry. But let's leave it now, Mab. Let's call a truce. I'll deal with Mother. Let's get that over and done with. Afterwards, we can come to blows about Leonie, if that's what you're after."

She winced, and he laughed, harshly and without humour.

"Well, we'll talk about it then. Perhaps blows won't be necessary. I'm sorry – an unfortunate expression."

She listened to him appalled. He seemed so calm. He clearly felt he was being generous and reasonable, magnanimously overlooking her unwarranted interference because she was worried and distressed. And but for mere chance, he would have killed a child. She knew she should try to bring the horror of it home to him, but she felt numb and empty, aware of the futility of trying, unequal to the task.

"Robert," she began, but he interrupted her angrily.

"Look," he said. "I'm sorry, but Leonie is my business. Nobody asked you to saddle yourself with her. What happened between us is entirely our affair, and just now I'm not prepared to discuss it.

"You say you are worried about Mother, you want me to sort it out for you. Well, all right, I will. But I'm not going to sit here and listen to one of your lectures. You're not fit to give one anyway. Just look at you! Go home and have a rest, Mary. Later there will be plenty of time to chew the whole mess over. But not now."

He got up decisively.

"I think this lunch party is more or less finished," he said. "But have some coffee if you want to. I'm going to get the bill."

He did not wait for her to answer, but turned on his heel, weaving deftly away between the crowded tables.

Mary sat and watched him dully, automatically putting the compact back in her bag, groping for her gloves and coat.

He had found the table where Signor Molocco was sitting and was almost swinging on it, taking his weight on his fists. He seemed to be having a huge success there, she could hear the rise in the tempo of talk and laughter. Someone was already coming back from the kitchen with a clean glass and another carafe of wine. She was no longer the centre of attention; the roles had switched and the new audience would undoubtedly be more appreciative. By now he had probably forgotten all about her.

But as she reached the door he turned round and glanced at her challengingly, as if daring her to reprove him. The glass in his hand caught the sun and sparkled, and he held it up as if to toast her.

She looked at the bright glass and the bright face bleakly, unable for once to respond. He put the wine down with a shrug and turned back to the Italians, making some kind of joke, presumably, for there was a roar of laughter from the table; and as she shut the door behind her, he derisively blew her a kiss.

# 11

Stella knelt on a chair before the washbasin in her bathroom and gazed at the etching she had hung on the wall. She hoped it was safely fixed in position; it had been much heavier than she had expected, and the nail on which she had hung it had been so awkwardly placed, at precarious full-stretch across the expanse of porcelain. There had been painful moments, fiddling with the cord, trying to loop it over the unseen support while bearing the weight of the frame, and she had feared several times that she would drop it, shattering the glass and damaging the picture, creating an embarrassing mess that she would not have the strength to clear up alone. But there it was, she had managed it. She looked at it now with mingled satisfaction and apology. It would certainly prove a consolation, but it seemed a shame to relegate an old friend to so poor a place. The paper was already yellowed, steam and damp would do it no good. Well, at least you are only an etching, she told herself in an effort to ease the responsibility she felt towards it. Somewhere there are others like you; you're only unique in that I sincerely need you. You should be proud of such a sacrifice.

She climbed carefully down from the chair, glancing spitefully at the looking glass, displaced by her labours. It leant against the bath, ineffectually reflecting the cracks on the vacant shiny ceiling, shorn of its power to shock and depress. Even when she approached it, it failed to disclose anything but her legs, still firm and slender. Small feet. Neat ankles. She looked at them in surprise, astonished to find them untouched by the devastating effects of her illness, taken aback by their spry, almost jaunty shapeliness.

She was not vain; too many things had been important, engrossing, to allow time for vanity. Beside the urge, the ability to create, her appearance had seemed of little consequence. She knew she had been born, if not beautiful, then with a face and bearing that pleased the eye, and she was thankful for it, as one is thankful for the warmth of the sun or the greenness of the grass. She clothed and groomed herself efficiently and automatically, much as she tended her house, or the plants in the garden, faintly resentful of the time and energy it all demanded, but acknowledging that it was a necessary chore. You cannot live in a slum or allow yourself to become unkempt and neglected. Some effort must be squandered in the name of proper pride. Besides, it was a pleasant bonus to be found attractive, and the power to enchant often proved surprisingly useful. But there was not time to dwell upon such things; in her scale of values they were relatively unimportant.

She had not given much thought to the onset of old age, had not counted the grey hairs or noticed the wrinkles. Life had been too full, and its quality did not depend on chestnut curls, on the smoothness of skin, on the elasticity of a muscle. Charm, in the sense that it was hers, did not seem affected by the loss of these things either; she had not been conscious of any lessening of her ability to please, to influence, to impress. It would have seemed ridiculous to mourn the inevitable changes in her body, so natural and gentle, when there was still so much to absorb her and hold her attention.

No, she thought, still mysteriously held by the sight of her legs in the discarded mirror. No. I've never been distressed by the fact that I am ageing. I hardly noticed it; it was unimportant. It didn't, it wouldn't have, worried me at all.

She bent suddenly and picked up the looking glass, turning it to the wall with a hurried violent gesture, blotting out the image of her graceful calves, her delicate ankles. It shamed her that she should be pained by the sight of them, that suddenly she should be riven with longing to be the whole, fresh, youthful Stella who would once have smiled back at her from the lifted glass.

"It should not matter," she said aloud to the empty bathroom. "It has never mattered. I have never grieved for what I used to be, or flinched from looking glasses. I have always thought it farcical to resist old age."

Her hand ached where she had knocked it against the basin and her eyes fell vaguely upon it as she spoke. There, as if to refute her words, she saw the dark stain spreading, purple below the fine transparent skin, unnaturally large, a bruise out of all proportion to the injury. She stared at it in disgust. No, this was not old age, this thing she faced. Old age was leisurely and dignified, an almost imperceptible pattern of change. But this . . . this was eerie, shattering . . . a hideously accelerated ruin. It was as if the clock that governed the normal run down of her body had been wound up by some madman so that she raced crazily towards decomposition, crumbling, rotting before her own eyes. Her breast, which putrified as if she was already in her coffin, her hair, now starting to fall out in handfuls from the effects of her treatments. No, she need not be ashamed to recoil from the sight of such destruction.

"Why should I watch it?" she said to the mirror. "Why should I start each day staring at death?"

She glanced up at the etching, seeking comfort from its familiarity, from its air of ordered calm. Winter trees, austere and simple, in a landscape almost bleak in its severity; to Stella the restraint was reassuring. There was no extravagance here and no confusion. You could see that in time Spring would come to those trees; they would bud and grow green again just as nature had intended. Nothing chaotic or untoward would afflict them; they were sane, normal, regulated.

Yes, she was glad that she had hung the etching here. This was where she needed its sanity, above the monotonous white enamel of the basin before which she seemed to spend such aeons of time. It was bad enough to sway there daily, coughing, retching, clinging to the porcelain, without having to contend with her own reflection. Perhaps this stern winter landscape would give her strength as she stood there, rigid with rejection, glass in one hand and pills in another. Maybe it would make them easier to swallow.

She moved the chair back against the wall and sank down upon it. She sat limply, loosely, her arms hanging by her sides. She would surrender to the fatigue; let it seep through her, befogging her will, blurring her reactions. But the effort of undressing, of making ready for the night, was too enormous to contemplate.

Her thoughts drifted back over the long taxing day that had begun as it was finishing, here in this bathroom. How had she endured it? Had she really been to the hospital, seen Dr. Zuckerman, got herself home again? Had she spoken to workmen, supervised the arrival of the garden seat, eaten a meal with Leonie? Had she conversed with people in a rational fashion, presenting a normal, even cheerful, appearance? And still had the strength to come up here and wrestle with a mirror and a picture? It scarcely seemed possible. Other days were lying ahead, to be lived through and dealt with according to their demands upon her. Where would she find the will and the courage? She almost wept with exhaustion at the thought of them.

She stared groggily across the floor at the door that led to her bedroom. Henry. Henry would help her. She could see his face come round it puzzled and a little anxious. 'Stella, what on earth are you doing? Why have you shut yourself up in the lavatory?'

What would he think if he saw her like this, craven, eroded with self-pity, sitting slumped in a chair? 'Where do you get your energy from?' he used to say. 'It makes me feel giddy. Can't you sit still for a moment?' But she knew he loved her vitality, was proud of her stamina. He must not find her like this. Abruptly, she straightened her spine, pulled her feet back under her.

After all, it had been something of a triumph, the lack of fear she had felt today at the hospital. Today Dr. Zuckerman had lost his omnipotence; he was no longer a god, with power to reprieve or destroy her. He had shrunk to size, had become what she supposed he always had been, a diligent but unimaginative consultant, with a face so ordinary that in any other context she would have found it completely unmemorable. How could she ever have found his lack of expression sinister, the banality of his features inhuman? For the first time she noticed how small he was, smaller than the nurse in the crackling starched apron, and the discovery made her feel almost sorry for him; she too was small, and had learnt recently to fear the commanding height of nurses. But then, that had been ridiculous too, for today she could see that despite their size, the nurses were quite insignificant: kind, nondescript girls with thick legs and more responsibility than they could courteously handle, condemned to work in a concrete cave from which she, Stella, would soon be free.

Indeed she was already free. It was only her hope that had chained her to this hospital, that had made it terrible to her. She realised now that until today she had never quite given up the buried childish fantasy that some miracle might indeed reverse her illness. The clammy chill she had felt before seeing Dr. Zuckerman had in fact been the chill of unbearable suspense. Today she at last found herself empty of hope, and with its passing, the nightmare had simply evaporated. There was nothing here any longer to hold her in thrall, nothing that could be given or withheld from her, no prospect of mercy, of remission or cure. Sitting in the familiar waiting room, walking along the corridors, stepping through the doors where once her heartbeats had hammered in her eardrums, she felt she had awakened from a long bout of delirium. Here was no sorcerer's lair, peopled by zombies, ruled by an incubus, but an ugly busy hospital, filled with ugly busy doctors. Soon she would see one of them, and he would tell her that he could do nothing more for her. That was all. There was no longer anything of which to be afraid.

In the past she had only been dimly aware of the patients with whom she shared the purgatory of the waiting room. She had seen them, not as people, but as an amorphous frieze of misery round the walls, as much part of the place as the chairs they sat on. She had been afraid of them too, afraid to look into their faces and find her own terror reflected, afraid to find in the sight of their panic confirmation of her own.

Today, secure in the citadel of her new hopelessness, she watched them deliberately. They sat in rows, as if lined up for her inspection, clear-cut against the shiny paint; it was as if some grotesque fresco to which she had unconsciously become accustomed had suddenly burst into life. The faces could have

116

been painted to show every stage of human adversity, from the first incredulous shock, through every level of diminishing hope into despair. You could pick out the new patients at a glance. This time it was a youth of perhaps eighteen, in dirty jeans and a black studded jacket, a crutch flung down indignantly beside his bandaged leg. Not yet disciplined by the stunned hush in the waiting room, he seemed set on conversation; anxious to explain that he had been brought there under false pretences; desperate to reinforce his determination that a foolish mistake had been made.

"It's only a knock," he said, leaning aggressively over the unresponsive figure beside him. "Nothing the matter with it, only came here to please my mum, see? Tell you, I won't be back here in a hurry, no fear! Not me! Doctors . . ."

He swore, scornfully but uneasily, as if daring the medical profession to confirm such an absurd diagnosis, and looked round the silent circle, appealing for support. His face was very white, perhaps in contrast to his hair which was dyed in curious hues, with tufts of red and orange; under it his child's eyes stared out, feverish and stricken, belying the bravado of the rich obscenities.

Stella's eyes had fallen to the man beside him, who had remained motionless, as if deaf to the tirade. Yes, she could see he had been coming here much longer, but not long enough to have anything left over from his own inward battle. He sat stiffly to attention, his eyes fixed on a spot somewhere on the opposite wall. Above the neat line of his collar she could see the purple mark of the radiotherapist's pencil; something wrong with his throat then, perhaps he did not speak because he could not; but the woman on the boy's other side leant forward and murmured something to him which seemed to hit the right note, for he lounged back on his seat again, his diseased leg thrust out before him, his thumbs stuck carelessly in his pockets.

What did she find to say to him, wondered Stella, remembering the ill-assorted pair and how they had continued to talk together. She must have known instinctively how to calm him down and yet not puncture the pathetic bubble of his nonchalance. What did she say? I would not have known how to begin, distanced from him by the punk haircut, by the oaths and the insolence, by every superficial habit of thought and behaviour, and yet I understood exactly what he was feeling. I have been there, in the same welter of disbelief, of outrage and resentment. I could have helped him if I had the humanity to overcome my stultifying inhibitions. Here I am, at the end of a long life that has been full and privileged and rewarding, and I cannot find the words to comfort a terrified boy.

She opened her eyes, disgusted with herself and yet suddenly stronger, as if her pity and remorse had generated their own bitter energy. Before her, on the further side of the room, the medicine cupboard swam into focus, and she went to it angrily, wrenching the door open with a jerk that sent Dr. Zuckerman's chart fluttering from its shelf into her face. She did not attempt to catch it but watched it fall, spinning round and round in the up-draught from the radiator like some huge ungainly moth, until it flapped itself to rest in the bath.

She looked down at it wonderingly, resisting the impulse to rush and rescue it from the dripping tap. It had meant so much to her, the written recipe for hope, the magic spell that might bring health and happiness. She had learnt its pattern by heart, but still she had kept it carefully lest, like some feckless heroine of a fairy-tale, she should forget the wizard's words and perish.

Now the wizard had changed his mind, had countermanded his instructions. The chart, for all its impressive display of coloured stickers and officious little boxes, had become nothing more than an outdated piece of paper, empty of meaning or promise. Empty. Like the face of Dr. Zuckerman and the expressions he used with such complacency . . . contra-indications . . . alternative thinking . . . reassessment of progress . . . Did she understand, he kept asking, did she understand? Further treatment by chemotherapy was, for the moment, out of the question. Did she understand? It would certainly cause an alarming deterioration in her condition.

An alarming deterioration in her condition. How adroitly he could navigate his way around the forbidden words. It was a perfect phrase and indeed she understood it.

She bent and picked the chart from the bath, crumpling it savagely in her hand. It should make no difference, she thought. I have known for a long time that the drugs would kill me. I have been deliberately misleading that doctor. What difference is there between deluding him, and acting against his advice and authority? None. And yet yesterday I still consulted the chart; there was a tiny part of me that still pretended I was doing my best to get better, obeying doctor's orders, behaving with good sense: but tonight I am just killing myself. Committing suicide. Practising euthanasia. How ugly, how melodramatic, it all sounds. Henry would not like to hear me speak like that. Perhaps, after all, Dr. Zuckerman's way is best; better to think of it cloaked in his genteel evasive phrases. Tonight I am hastening an alarming deterioration in my condition.

She bit her lip, peering into the cabinet. Yes, there was surely an adequate supply. Doctors always over-prescribed; she used to think it deplorable waste as she threw away the costly remains of cough-mixtures, of painkillers and children's sedatives, but now it turned out to be a dispensation from the gods. The loathsome little bottles were half-full, lethal and dependable. No doubt they would see her out, and if they looked like failing her, why then she could double, quadruple, the dose. Why not? She could take them all tonight. Why not?

She looked again at the bruise on her hand, at the way the skin stretched, fragile between the sinews. Why not indeed? Only because of Mary. Only because of the words that would not come, of the gestures still to be made. She remembered again the boy at the hospital. She could have helped him, could at least have answered him; but she had let him go, half swaggering, half limping from the room; passing out of her life as so many had before him, no contact made, no comfort given. She had failed so many times, strangers, acquaintances, friends, Julia, Mary. But she would not fail Mary. She would take her pills as usual, so that later, afterwards, everything would seem more natural. Better they should not know; it would only add to their distress. But she would do no more until she had somehow crossed the barrier to Mary, made some confession, some declaration. Perhaps tomorrow she would know what to do.

She took the bottles in her hand, flooded with irrational relief. Am I so afraid then, she thought? Afraid of the void, of extinction in the dark? Yes. But that is nothing beside the fear of living. It will be swift and clean; I will be free of this obscenity, of this decay.

She crossed to the basin, disturbed by her elation. The darkness of the night and the struggle of the morning lay black before her, and yet she felt as though she had been reprieved. It was good to think that tomorrow she would see the river; would walk in the studio; would find an echo of Henry in the carving she had fashioned. It was good that she might still snatch joy from all that she cherished; she could touch her chisels; listen to music. She might see Robert, hear the lilt of his voice, what richness, what satisfaction! She was even glad that she could finish the book that she was reading.

She measured the pills carefully, two from this bottle, one from that. She might have time to feel the strength creep into the white winter sunlight; to smell the warmth in the earth. Anything was possible.

She filled the glass and swallowed effortlessly, her eyes fixed on the winter trees, lifeless and bare before her. Tenderly, gingerly, she reached out and touched the etching. Soon the black twigs would bud. Perhaps she would live to see it happen.

She dropped her hands, smiling, and leant on the basin, while in front of her she watched the picture blossom, verdant and irrepressible, green with the leaves of Spring.

# 12

Mary walked along the narrow pavement beside the little park that separated her terrace from the embankment. The street lamps were old and dim there, and between their pools of light and the glare and flash of the main road on the farther side the gardens lay darkly, black and mysterious.

A small boy passed her, dragging back on his mother's hand. He was running a stick along the railings – clack, clack, clack – as she had done so often in her own childhood; peering through the uprights at the familiar trees made strange by the night; unwilling to exchange them for the tame world of the nursery; shuffling her feet in the leaves, reluctant to hurry, to respond to Stella's fretful urging, 'Come along, Mary. Come *along*! Whatever are you doing?'

When she was quite small she had been given one of those advent calendars, designed to be lit from behind, with little windows that you opened, one each day. After that, it had been particularly difficult to leave the pavement after darkness, for the terrace was so exactly like an advent calendar – windows lit behind the concealing curtains; intriguing chinks of light showing through the cracks of shutters, along the edges of blinds. But the lit rooms, though the most tantalising, seldom fulfilled their promise; in the early evening curtains, once pulled, usually remained shut. It was better to concentrate on the black windows, where if you were lucky a light might suddenly leap out, making you jump in surprise, illuminating a whole astonishing world within. You would stare at it, enthralled by the brilliance of the revelation, desperate to see it all quickly, because you had only an instant to drink it in. Only an instant before a figure would appear, silhouetted against the vivid tableau behind it, and draw a curtain sharply and brutally over the picture, blotting out the magical scene, leaving you bereft in the dark. 'Come *along*, child,' Stella would cry, leaning bored and exasperated on the handle of Robert's push-chair. 'What are you doing, dawdling and gaping? Hurry up, do!'

She had never told Stella that the terrace was an advent calendar; that it was enormously important – quite essential to her peace of mind – to see one window lit up each night. A pity, because she could see now that it was the sort of obsession Stella might have understood. But Stella had not seemed understanding on those winter afternoon excursions. Mary had felt very early that only a sense of duty towards the children prompted her to make them. For Stella herself they had been exhausting and tiresome, a waste of precious time. Stiff with suppressed irritation she had dragged them along behind her, through endless parks and round interminable duckponds, pushing them on swings; feeding bread to the pigeons, irked alike by Robert's ceaseless energy and Mary's own incurable tendency to stare and loiter. She had dashed between them, inept and frustrated, capturing the fleeing Robert, looking back to where Mary stood, lost in contemplation of some new marvel. 'Come along, Mary, do! For good-ness sake. . .'

Poor Stella. Her sporadic efforts to be an involved mother had not been very successful. And yet she had tried – and had gone on trying. She had taken them swimming and trailed them round museums; had taught them to play the piano; had bought tickets for the circus and attended school concerts. But Mary had always been able to tell when her boredom and impatience were becoming unendurable. She had a particular way of sitting at such times, very neat and straight, but leaning forward slightly and balanced on the edge of the chair with her hands clenched on the front of the seat on either side of her thighs, her chin thrust slightly forward. It was as if she hoped that by making herself as uncomfortable as possible she could at least give herself something to think about other than the tedium of the pantomime; of the sports day; of the pedantic sales assistant who was taking all afternoon to fit their school clothes.

At least Robert gave her something back, thought Mary. I

gave her nothing. I spoke in monosyllables, never venturing a subject for conversation, paralysed by the knowledge of how dull she found me, unwilling to offer more of myself in case that was found wanting too. I never saw that it was my reticence that made me so depressingly unrewarding; that I could have done much to alleviate the unfortunate fact that I was a child by showing promise that one day I might be a more stimulating companion, like Robert. Even as a baby Robert had been able to make her laugh; had made it clear that he would turn out to be intelligent and amusing. He must have been difficult, exhausting to handle, but at least there could never have been any doubt about the strength of his personality. But I was just a dead weight, trailing along behind her, mute and introverted; admiring her so much and unable to show it; growing slowly bitter; building up an indestructible shield of reserve and resentment. Well, perhaps I needed it then, but why can't I break through it now that I want to? It's as if I'd absorbed the personality I created to shelter me.

Maybe I should try to talk to her more about the early days, she thought. Perhaps that would be a beginning. It might make things clearer for both of us. But Stella was always reluctant to dwell on the past, especially since Father died. It was as if she could not bear to remember. If only I could time it right, she thought, if I could catch her in a mellow mood, like that time last summer when I found out about Robert.

She had come home that day to find Stella in her study, sorting out a drawer of old letters. She had spread out a selection of photographs on the desk before her and seemed completely absorbed in them, her back turned to the door. Mary advanced hesitantly, clearing her throat to make her presence obvious, not wishing to pry or intrude.

But that time Stella had been pleased to see her; had turned towards her gaily with a photograph extended for her to see.

"Look at this," she said, smiling. "What a fat little thing you were in those days, Mary! Don't we all look ridiculous?"

It was not a formal photograph, more of a snapshot really, but somehow the figures were formal, as if the occasion was special and the participants ill at ease. Father, grave and neat, but apparently proud as a peacock, holding by the hand a fat surly child in a party frock of great magnificence – herself; she remembered the dress, but could not recall when she had worn it. And, on his other arm, Stella, looking alarmed and yet curiously radiant, very pregnant in an elegant flowing gown and holding a bunch of flowers with a spray of ferns arranged around them.

Mary had laughed; they did look ridiculous, so posed and uncomfortable as if someone had insisted that they be photographed.

"What were we doing?" she asked. "We look as if we were at a wedding!"

"Well, of course we were," said Stella in astonishment. "Don't you remember, Mary? We were at our own wedding – your father's and mine!"

Mary looked again at the photograph. Surely it couldn't just be the dress? But no; not even allowing for a radical change in fashion. The bride, if that was truly Stella's role on this occasion, was undoubtedly expecting a baby.

She felt stunned.

"But you're pregnant!" she blurted out before she could stop herself. "It can't be your wedding! Look – see!" she tapped the photograph emphatically. "You are obviously expecting Robert. . ."

"Of course I am," said Stella calmly. She took the snapshot from Mary's drooping hand and replaced it on the pile before her.

"Surely you knew that, Mary? Gracious me, how long do you think it takes to have a baby? I know you were small, but even so, you can't have failed to notice that Robert was born a few months after we were married. And it all happened in such a rush too. Why did you think we decided things so quickly?"

Quickly? Then it really had been a sudden decision. Not, as she had thought, a long-standing arrangement like other people's weddings; a grown-up conspiracy, deliberately, artfully concealed.

"But I didn't think it was quickly arranged," she said wonderingly, remembering with surprising immediacy the ache of her wounded pride and the sickening sensation of exclusion. "I thought that you had decided it long before. That you had left me out . . . not bothered to tell me."

"But, Mary!" interrupted Stella in obvious amazement. "We *did* tell you! Of course we told you we had decided it suddenly. And I can't remember for certain, but I should think we told you why."

"Then I simply didn't believe you," Mary answered slowly. "I thought you just let me know of your plans at the last moment. Because I did not matter. Because you were indifferent to what I felt about it. I thought you had arranged it all behind my back; that everyone knew before I did.

"That was the reason, the only reason, really, that I was so upset when you married Father. That was why I was so angry. Why I made such a fuss. Surely you remember?"

Stella nodded, staring at her in dismay, her chin cupped in her hand. Of course she would not have forgotten; the tears and the moping; the throwing off of advances; the sulking and the resentment. She had been impossible, the archetype of the difficult child of a former marriage.

"It was because I thought I had been left out," she repeated, suddenly anxious, after all these years, to excuse the sullen far-away child who had behaved so disgracefully. "I was terribly hurt and offended. I thought you simply hadn't bothered."

"Oh dear," said Stella helplessly. "Oh dear me. How awful!"

She sat back in her chair, rumpling her hair wildly with both hands, peering out under the resultant tangle in real distress. Watching her, Mary was filled with a rush of tenderness. She looked funny and somehow touching under the spiky halo, not much changed from the glowing young woman in the photograph. Most elderly ladies are neatly brushed and combed, she thought, and do not have ink-blots on their fingers; they do not disarrange their coiffeurs, some of them even wear hairnets. The picture of Stella in a hairnet was so pleasingly incongruous that she found herself smiling. Unselfconsciousness was such an essential part of Stella; no wonder it had reappeared

125

to an exaggerated degree in Robert. But it accounts for a lot of your charm, thought Mary. It makes you seem so ridiculously young.

"As I recall it," she was saying, "you were the only person we DID bother about. I remember how nervous we both were of telling you – because you were so close, so important to Henry. I thought you were just jealous, that you hated me for encroaching on your relationship with your father."

"Hated you?" exclaimed Mary, aghast. "You thought I hated you? But that's nonsense. It wasn't like that at all."

I worshipped you, she wanted to say. At the age of five I worshipped you. I thought you were – fabulous. Stella. A star. So beautiful, so bewitching, so unattainable. That's how I thought of you when I was little.

But she couldn't say that; it sounded exaggerated, absurd.

"I never hated you," she went on at last. "Not for a moment. But you seemed . . . oh . . . so superior and un-approachable." She groped for words, aware that as usual she was sounding inadequate.

But for once Stella seemed to comprehend, to see through the understatement. She began to tell her about her marriage to Henry; about the belated discovery of an unwanted pregnancy; of her sudden change of heart; how Henry, determined not to lose a moment, had secured a special licence; how they really had married at a few days' notice. And in the end, how thankful she had been that it had all happened, how in some obscure fashion she had always felt indebted to Robert for her happiness.

Sitting in the fading light, understanding for the first time that the adults who had so offended her had intended no slight, had laid no plans to belittle or exclude her, she felt close to Stella as she had not felt in years. It was all so long ago, it should not matter any longer, yet she felt absurdly warmed and comforted.

Why didn't it last, she wondered, remembering how inexorably the feeling of closeness had faded; how they had become wary again as the moment of intimacy had grown dim. Yes, perhaps she should try to persuade Stella to talk more about the past. It might help with the present.

She was almost opposite the house now and she glanced up at it anxiously, edging between the parked cars that lined the narrow road. She could see the hall lamp glow through the fanlight, but the window of Stella's study was in darkness. Well, it was late – late for Stella, anyway. She had looked at her watch as she waited to cross the embankment and even then it had been after ten o'clock. She has probably gone to bed, thought Mary guiltily. I wouldn't have gone out last night if I had known C.D. would keep me so long this evening.

It was not unusual for two days to pass without her seeing Stella, but tonight she was haunted by the last glimpse she had had of her, wraith-like and haggard on the landing above. She felt a stab of panic; what if something should have happened to Stella since she had last spoken to her? But that's ridiculous, she told herself firmly; I'm exaggerating the whole thing, letting my imagination run away with me. After all, if she needs me she has only to lift the telephone. No one can say she's ever held back from disturbing me at the office.

She smiled to herself in the darkness, remembering an untold number of ill-timed 'phone calls, no reason to interrupt her was judged too trivial by Stella. Would she pick up Father's trousers from the cleaners? Could she call at the gallery on the way home and see if the carvings had been arranged as she suggested? Did she know where on earth yesterday's paper had got to, there was such an interesting article in it, and she wanted to show it to Robert? 'I can't talk now,' she would shout, 'I'm right in the middle of a conference. I keep telling you not to ring me up like this at the office.' But it had never made any difference. That time she had lost the newspaper, for instance, she had come through again before the meeting was finished to say that she had found it behind the log box. No, if Stella had needed her she would surely have telephoned. It was foolish to worry on that score. Still, it would certainly have been reassuring to have got home early this evening. How like C.D. to have chosen this moment for his interminable run-through of her presentation.

She let herself into the hall without enthusiasm. Stella would have gone to bed; and she herself, what would she do in the silent house? Make herself a snack in the kitchen, perhaps, and see if there was anything on television? After a long day she knew she would usually have found such a prospect relaxing, but tonight the thought of it brought no pleasure. She was tired all right, but she was more than just tired; she was worried and unsettled and lonely.

It was not until she was putting the chain on the heavy door that she realised the house was not silent. She could hear voices coming from the library, and the light shone out from behind the turn of the stairwell. Stella must be in there after all, listening to the radio or looking at television herself. How lovely that she had not gone to bed. They could talk by the fire; have a nightcap together. She ran down the hallway and put her head round the library door.

"I'm back," she said, struggling with the buttons of her overcoat. "I thought I'd never get away from the office."

The voices in the room ceased abruptly as she spoke. Looking up, she saw that Stella's chair was empty and that Leonie, already on her feet, was standing in front of the sofa. Leonie. Of course. How could she have forgotten about Leonie? Somebody was with her too, a short stocky man she had not seen before. He had fair hair and his face was too fat. She was sure he reminded her of someone, but for the moment she could not find the connection.

She stared at them coldly. She felt baulked and disappointed, perversely annoyed by the polite way they stood to greet her. They looked so settled and domestic, like a couple disturbed by an unexpected caller. They will be offering me a chair next, she thought crossly. I feel like an intruder in my own house.

"Where's Stella?" she asked sharply. "She's not in the study. I looked there as I came in."

She threw her coat on a chair and crossed to the drinks tray, turning her back rudely on the unknown man. She would pour herself a whisky. A large one. Much larger than usual. She picked up the bottle angrily and screwed off the lid.

"Stella's gone to bed," Leonie was saying behind her. "She said to tell you she would see you tomorrow evening, that she had had a long day. She looked, she was very tired, I think."

Her voice petered out and Mary did not answer. She felt alarmed by her own irritation, and by the inclination she felt to bully these harmless yet subtly infuriating people. I feel like Robert, she thought, splashing water into the hefty drink in the tumbler. Is it something to do with Leonie? Her voice? The way she stands? And the man. She glanced at him with distaste. He looked smug and prosperous; someone should tell him to avoid pink shirts with that complexion.

"I don't think we have met," she said aloud, forcing out the pleasantry with an effort.

Leonie came forward at once, like a dog, thought Mary, encouraged by a kind word. Still, now that she saw her closer, there was no mistaking that she had been improved by the arrival of her visitor. For the first time the listlessness that had enveloped her had lifted, and now that her eyes were alive again they dominated her small face. Huge gentle eyes, brown and glistening – to Mary they did not seem quite human; they looked more as if they belonged to one of those small tree-climbing animals, lemurs were they? Or some sort of monkey? But perhaps that was unkind. At any rate you could not deny that Leonie's eyes were in their way beautiful.

"I'm sorry," she was saying eagerly. "I should have . . . I didn't get a chance to introduce you. Mary, this is Johnny, Johnny Morris. And. . ."

She turned to her companion with the air of a conjuror producing a rabbit from a hat – "this is Mary, Johnny. I was speaking of her only a moment ago. This is Robert's sister, Mary!"

Johnny stared at her without affection, and all at once she saw herself mirrored in his eyes. Robert's stance, Robert's hair, Robert's ill manners, the brimming glass in her hand.

"Yes," he said at last. "Yes. Of course. I can see that."

His voice was flat and good-humoured and yet in some way the words were not meant to be friendly. She felt she was being asked to deny her affinity to the outlawed spirit of Robert. Until then, a sister who resembled him to such an unfortunate degree could hardly expect to be trusted. Yet she knew the partnership was on offer, could be had for the asking; three against one, cosy and respectable and disapproving, and Robert, whose home this was, not even there to defend himself. She would not, could not, do it.

She looked stonily back at Johnny. Placid and fair, plump hands like a baby . . . a baby. . . That was what he reminded her of. He reminded her of Toby.

"Yes," she said, almost unconsciously mimicking his manner of speech. "And you must be Toby's father. Of course. I can see that too."

She perched herself on the arm of Stella's chair and sealed her allegiance with a smile that she knew was purely Robert, a gesture that extended to the mouth only, while the eyes were kept empty, insolent in their contradiction of the social grimace below them. It was an expression that they had perfected together in their childhood and it had been a useful weapon, though she could not remember when she had last used it. But Robert had no such scruples – everyone from angry schoolmasters to hostile critics had in turn been withered by The Smile; it was so palpably insincere, and yet its politeness could not be called into question. Only Stella was proof against it. 'Don't smirk at me in that horrible manner,' she would say deflatingly. But Johnny was not Stella. He was only a fat man in a shirt that matched his face to perfection.

He retrenched at once, as she knew he would – dropping his eyes before The Smile; retreating into confusion. Even Leonie, seeing Robert rise unexpectedly before her, looked startled; no, more than startled, stricken. Well, so she should, thought Mary uncharitably, taking another mouthful of whisky. Just because she prefers fat men in pink shirts doesn't mean Robert is dead and buried. Without offering them a drink, she deliberately recharged her glass.

"Mary," Leonie was saying pleadingly. "Johnny has come to say that he thinks that for Toby's sake . . . that for all our sakes . . . we should try to . . . well, forget about what has happened. He doesn't want to make any trouble, but he thinks, and I think too, that it has all been a dreadful mistake, this . . . this interlude, with Robert. He wants us to go away with him."

130

Mary did not answer but took a generous gulp from her glass as if it was the cocoa she would much rather have been sharing with Stella.

"You've both been so kind," Leonie went on. "You have. And Mrs. Leonard. But she is not well, Mary. You must know that. She's not fit to have us here. She hardly knows who we are sometimes; today she kept calling me Julia. . . And as for Robert. . ."

For the first time her voice wavered.

"I'm doing him no good, Mary. We have never been right for each other. I tried so hard, but nothing I can say, nothing I do, pleases him any longer. I think he only wants me around because he doesn't want me to be the one who does the leaving. I would go back, but can't you see, it would be hopeless? Sooner or later. . ."

She paused, and turned wretchedly to Johnny as if aware that these were not exactly the words he would want to hear. But he came forward and put his arm protectively around her shoulders, apparently unconscious of the fact that she had just declared herself unrequitedly in love with someone else.

"Leonie has had a bad time with your brother, Mary," he said, stiffly. "You know that, of course, and there's no point in my discussing it. But from now on I'm going to see that she is happy and properly cared for. What's past is past. Her welfare and Toby's, that's all I'm interested in now."

"And what were you interested in before?" said Mary, nastily. "When Leonie was having your baby, for instance? When Robert took them in and made a home for them?"

They are right, she thought. Why do I speak so meanly, so unkindly? What possible future could there be for Robert and a sad little waif like this, whom he should never have allowed to love him? She'll be far happier with her pompous simple-minded Johnny. Of course she must go, and serve Robert right, if some perversity still makes him want her.

"I'm sorry . . ." she began, but Leonie was already speaking.

"It wasn't Johnny's fault," she said. "He wanted to marry

131

me when he heard about . . . about Toby. He wanted to look after us, right from the beginning."

"Of course," said Mary quickly, and Johnny patted her again, a trifle more brusquely. But there was no stopping her now that she was started.

"It was then, when I didn't know what to do, when I didn't know where to turn, that I first got to know Robert. Oh, I'd seen him about – he'd even said once that he would like to paint me – but I'd never really tried to talk to him before. And then one day I met him by the river. It was like a dream – that's what it was like, Mary! I was so . . . so desperate, and he seemed to be really interested in me, to want to get to know me better. Afterwards, I realised that something bad had happened to him; that he was unhappy himself and just wanted someone to divert him. But at the time I didn't know that, and it all seemed marvellous. As if that was what I had been waiting for – what it had all been leading up to. . ."

She was really crying now, and she seemed oblivious of Johnny's restraining arm, still wrapped around her.

"He's not like anyone else, Mary," she said. "He's so strange, so exciting, different from anyone I've ever known. When he is happy it's as if a light shone from him. I . . . I can't explain it, but everything around him is brighter."

She lifted her hands to her eyes as if to blot out a radiance she no longer found endurable.

"But I can't make him shine like that any more," she said. "I can't make him happy like he was at the beginning. And now I'm afraid of him it's worse. Worse. Hopeless."

"I know," interrupted Mary. "I know."

What was she doing, standing there as if mummified, allowing Johnny to hear all this? After all, to her it was hardly a revelation. Other people – too many other people, not necessarily those that loved him – had been scorched by the fire that burnt in Robert; and most of them had described it more coherently. But in the end it came to the same thing; friends, patrons, mistresses; finally they gave up the struggle. They shook themselves free as Leonie must do now – must do this minute – before her friend in the pink shirt had time to realise what a dreary haven he represented.

She banged her glass down on the table and launched herself upon Leonie, taking her by the shoulders, determined at any cost to stop the spate of words.

"I know," she said again. "I know what it was like, but it's over now. It's finished. It was wrong for you anyway; you were trying to live out a fantasy; it was something that should never have happened."

She looked up at Johnny, seeking for support, and he nodded approvingly. He looked slightly dazed, but more, she suspected, at the sudden support from the enemy than because he had registered anything that Leonie had been saying.

"You go off with Johnny," she continued firmly. "You need each other. And Toby, he needs you both. It will be for the best." She shook the shoulders gently. "You'll make out all right – you'll see. You will be happy together."

She had spoken loudly to silence Leonie, and Leonie was silenced. She faced her mutely, her shoulders limp and unresponsive beneath Mary's encouraging hands. The library lamp was tall and heavily shaded, and they stood together in the pool of light it cast as if caught in a spotlight on some insubstantial stage. The rest of the room seemed far off, lost in the shadow. We could be anywhere, thought Mary. We could be back on the barge.

Reluctantly, her eyes met Leonie's, and for a curious moment they were at one, isolated from a world of Johnnys by their joint anxiety; united by a mutual disquiet, a mutual distress.

"I'll look after Robert," said Mary softly. "It's easier for me. I can't do much good, but I'll be there. I always have been."

She dropped her hands; she did not want to drown in this unlooked-for communion. She glanced round, seeking Johnny, who was now leaning against the chimney piece. He had taken a pipe from his pocket and was cleaning it with the self-satisfied air of a man who knows when he must leave the girls alone together. The look of him jarred unbearably upon her; she felt a pressing desire to see the last of him. And Leonie, yes, Leonie too. She did not wish to be sucked into some harrowing post-mortem of a failed relationship with Robert.

"I'm sure you are right," she said, stepping back and stationing herself between them. "Why don't you pack up now? You could always move out this evening." Her own voice sounded strange to her, a hearty encouraging voice from which all overtones of Robert had abruptly vanished.

But Leonie, it appeared, was determined to say good-bye to Stella, and Johnny had one or two things to do to his flat to make ready for the baby. They would go in the morning, without indecent haste and in proper order.

It is probably for the best, thought Mary. I'd have to wake Stella early otherwise and tell her, before I left for the office.

"I'll say good-night now anyway," she said firmly. "I have a long day tomorrow, and I need some proper sleep. Besides, you must have such a lot to talk over together."

"Mary . . ." began Leonie uneasily, but Mary interrupted her with asperity. She would not, she absolutely refused to be drawn into more intimate discussion about her family.

"Good-bye, Leonie," she said cheerfully, "and good luck." She turned round to include Johnny. "The best of luck to both of you."

It wasn't enough. Leonie's stiff form, her lost eyes, the very bandages on her arm, accused her of insufficiency.

She stepped forward unwillingly and kissed her lightly on the cheek, hoping to convey some sense of relationship, some measure of farewell. But the gesture was empty; a meaningless social convention between strangers.

It was not enough; but what else could she say? She moved quickly to the door, avoiding the searching eyes.

# 13

Stella stood on the steps and waved with determination until the brake lights had disappeared round the end of the gardens and the car was out of sight. So that was the end of Leonie; she felt faintly ashamed that she should feel so pleased by her departure, but there it was. She sat down on the new garden seat and breathed deeply, revelling in the freedom of the empty house behind her. Well, almost empty, if you did not count Mrs. Hubbard. The front door was open and she could hear the bang of a brush on the wainscotting, the clatter of a dustpan. You did not need to count Mother Hubbard; that was the delightful thing about her. She knew her worth and how much she was relied upon; she did not need constant attention to reassure her. No doubt she still found them odd, but after all these years their oddities needed no apology, nor any concealment. No, there's not much Mother Hubbard doesn't know about us, thought Stella peacefully. She's been in on every crisis, since the children were little; and that was a long time ago.

A long time ago. Standing here on top of the steps . . . waving good-bye to the children . . . feeling the same sense of liberation, of release . . . the sensation of being unshackled from an enormous load.

I should have changed, Stella thought. I should have become more giving, more unselfish, but I know I would manage them no better today.

The old guilt swept through her; the old shame at the exhilaration she had felt when the children left in the morning. Why had the tenderness never been proof against the vexation? Robert, clattering round the house, unable to find his cap, his scarf, his schoolbag, the hall clock chiming – 'I'll have to get the car out, Robert. You're going to miss the bus.' And Mary, so often in tears at breakfast – about anything – nothing – a lost book, an uncompleted passage of homework, now only partly recovered, silent and pale, looking for all the world as if she was going to a torture chamber. 'Can't you take a piece of toast and eat it on the way, Mary? It's not good for you to go without your breakfast like this.' Oh, the worry, the irritation, the boredom of looking after children. Yet I loved them, she thought. That was why they had such power to disturb me; they filled my mind with their maddening ills and problems. When they were in the house, half my concentration was on them; I couldn't work; I felt no inspiration. Robert . . . Robert had understood; she knew he had never doubted the intensity with which she cared for him . . . but Mary?

"Never mind," Mary had whispered once, standing on tip-toe to kiss her as she finally hustled them out after some particularly trying commotion. "Never mind. We'll be gone in a minute and then you can start to be happy."

She shivered; it was cold on the bench, and the memory too was chilling. She got up stiffly and wandered back through the sunny hall into her study.

How had she answered her? She could not remember. With a joke probably, the safest reply to many of Mary's more penetrating remarks. But she had not forgotten the earnest face, or the ring of the child's voice offering the unpalatable truth – not as an accusation but in complete good faith – as a soothing thought to help her through the frustration of the moment. Mary had known herself to be an encumbrance, that her step-mother would feel relief when the door shut behind her. How could she have let the child observe, come to accept, such a thing?

She went to her desk, resolutely putting away all thought of the children. It was so long ago; such self-reproach was futile, almost morbid. She would not wallow in the failures of the past. Not today. Especially not this morning, when suddenly against all reason, contrary to all possible expectation, she felt better, stronger, than she had for a long time.

"There you are," she said to Henry, grave and dignified in his silver frame on the desk. "A few forbidden drugs and a good overdose of sleeping pills, and what's the result? A distinct . . . a distinct remission!" She had been going to say 'improvement' but Henry wasn't to be taken in by such exaggeration. Still, a remission was good enough. Even one morning was worth some jubilation. But the photograph remained impassive, and she looked at it with sudden disgust. "I shall put you away," she told it. "You are cold, unresponsive. You are not at all like Henry." She took it off the desk and stood staring at it with dissatisfaction, tilting it this way and that in her hands. No, Henry was not there. She would put it away; give it to Mary for her bedroom. Henry was more alive for her as he had been this morning, sitting at his chair at the head of the breakfast table. She had seen him so clearly, fussing about his coffee, meticulously folding and dividing the morning paper. She smiled, still warmed and comforted by the vivid quality of the vision.

There was a knock at the door and Mrs. Hubbard's face peered in.

"Oh," she said after a moment, "I'm sorry Mrs. Leonard – thought you had someone with you."

Her voice was unhurried and toneless; no inflection, no change of emphasis was there to help the stranger to an easy understanding of Mother Hubbard. You were handed the bare words and you had to make the most of them. But over the years Stella had learnt to interpret them instinctively, and this morning Mother Hubbard was feeling reproachful.

"I had your coffee made," she went on. "But I could hear you talking from the kitchen, I could. Didn't like to bring one cup in if you had company. But I'll fetch it now. You look as though you need it."

The face disappeared and Stella shut her eyes for a moment, bracing herself for the smell of the coffee-pot. How could she explain to Mother Hubbard that the smell of coffee, of tea, of all sorts of small consoling things that should have brought her pleasure had now become revolting to her? Dr. Zuckerman had dismissed such aversions lightly, as unimportant side-effects of his treatment; but to Stella they were not unimportant. There seemed to be so many of them; the smell of soap, of talcum powder; the scent of flowers; the aroma of coffee; the taste of almost every beverage that had ever pleased her: she could not get used to the fact that all these things had become nauseous. Each time she found herself distressed and disappointed anew.

Never mind; she would pour the coffee on the pot-plant in the corner. Nothing must spoil the gift of this peerless morning, a morning when for once the cough had remained dormant – when she had woken refreshed and swallowed her pills without a struggle. A morning when the millstone that was Leonie had broken free without any warning, and bowled away round the corner and out of her life in a yellow car driven by a plump man who looked just like Toby. How extraordinary, and how satisfactory! It was surely allowable to feel relieved that such a disturbing episode was over; to hope, at least, that it was over.

She drummed her fingers on the desk, annoyed that so much remained to perplex her. Nothing had been explained; the loose ends were still untied. Why, for instance, had Robert needed the devotion of such a dull little creature? And why, when her presence caused him such explosions of violence, could he not let her go? For, if she was to believe Leonie's distress – indeed, her fear – this morning, he still did not want her to leave him.

Her eyes fell to the piece of paper Leonie had given her; her new address and telephone number, written out in a careful school-girlish hand. She wished she had not asked her where she was going, after all, she had not cared to know, but at the time it had seemed impolite to show no interest in keeping in touch with her. Especially when the poor girl had appeared genuinely moved at the prospect of saying good-bye.

So she had asked, and Leonie had written the thing out readily enough. It was not until Stella was holding the paper that she suddenly seemed to regret it, and then she had behaved so strangely – begging her not to give it to Robert, or tell him where she could be found, obviously distraught at the very prospect – nearly in tears.

At the time, Stella had been surprised at the girl's alarm and vehemence; surprised and unsympathetic. Really, what an unnecessary fuss to make about Robert! And yes, it had irked her to see that Leonie imagined him determined to trace and contact her, when she herself only felt fear and repugnance at the thought. Yet she knew that was unfair. Robert had behaved in an inexcusable and alarming manner. She could not, of course, believe that he had tried to injure Toby, it was obscene to connect Robert, drunk or sober, with such barbarity, but he had undoubtedly broken Leonie's arm, and the child had been hurt, dropped in the struggle, most probably. It was ugly and horrible. No one could expect Leonie to want to continue that sort of relationship.

Well, she has my promise, thought Stella. As far as Robert is concerned, I don't know where to find her.

She folded the paper, frowning, and stuffed it absently into a pigeon hole in the desk. She was not used to having her word doubted, and Leonie had certainly been difficult to reassure. "I am not in the habit of betraying confidences," she had said in the end, rather coldly; and Leonie had coloured and apologised.

The subject had been dropped. But the girl's uneasiness still worried her.

"I must not tell Robert," she said aloud, as if speech would drive the matter home more forcibly. She was becoming so unlike herself these days, so muddled and vague. It would be terrible if Leonie's lack of faith in her were justified.

She felt a touch on her sleeve and started violently, but it was only Mother Hubbard. She was looking at her curiously, with an expression mid-way between anxiety and impatience, and Stella could smell the cup of coffee, poured and ready in her other hand.

"You all right, Mrs. Leonard?" she said. "You're in a proper day-dream this morning. I could stand here all day and I don't think you'd notice me."

"I brought your coffee," she went on. "And I'm cleared up early. Got everything neat and tidy in no time now our visitors have left us. So I thought I'd just run on now. But maybe you'd like me to stay around if you're not feeling too good today, Mrs. Leonard, would you? You only have to say, you know."

Stella shook her head, gripping the edge of the desk to support herself. Weakness and giddiness lapped over her in waves. All because Mother Hubbard made me jump, she thought crossly. Or perhaps it was the smell of the coffee.

"My, you do look peaky this morning! Here you are." Mrs. Hubbard pulled up a chair and Stella sank down in it gratefully. "And look, did you see that Miss Mary had left you a note before she went out to the office? She told me to make sure you didn't miss it."

"Why so she has," said Stella, surprised. "I hadn't noticed it. What ever would I do without you, Mother Hubbard? But I'm quite all right thank you. As a matter of fact, I was thinking how well I felt today. Not at all peaky, really. So do run along, and I'll see you tomorrow morning."

She did feel better now she was sitting down, but Mrs. Hubbard seemed unconvinced and lumbered ponderously about behind her, patting cushions and straightening lampshades.

"You should take a good rest, Mrs. Leonard," she said at last, stationing herself in front of Stella. "You've been taking too much out of yourself lately; I've seen you and I know. But now you've finished Mr. Leonard – and he's lovely, really, one of your best, if you don't mind my mentioning it – you should have a bit of a break, a bit of relaxation. Why don't you take yourself for a walk? It's lovely this morning, down by the river. Do you good to get a little fresh air for a change after all the dust in that studio."

Stella smiled at her with real affection. Dear Mother Hubbard, who perceived so much and yet so little about her. A long walk by the river, she might as well attempt a space flight. And yet how like her to have noticed the effort she had put into the carving and to accept without question the reappearance of her late employer disguised as a bird of prey. "Now that you've finished Mr. Leonard. . ."

Stella laughed with pleasure. "I'm glad you like him, Mother Hubbard," she said warmly. "I think he's good, but I've not shown him to anybody. He's a very private carving you see; a very personal carving. I've made him as a . . . as a sort of token really, a very special present.

"And now you must go off," she went on. "You really must. I'll be all right. I haven't felt fitter for ages."

She should have been an art critic, thought Stella, hearing the front door bang and the heavy footfalls die away along the pavement. She's got the feel all right; there's no fooling Mother Hubbard. Once, long ago, after Julia had died, when the buried guilt and sorrow were becoming impossible to endure, she had fashioned a gruesome carving, an abstract thing, blind and clawing, crying for help to a world grown deaf and distant. It had matured fast, fed by the fury of her grief and self-reproach; shaping itself in the mould of her pain and bitterness, and she had shown it to no one, not daring to expose her need for catharsis even to those who would have understood it; unable to show the thing to Robert; to Henry even. But Mrs. Hubbard had not counted. And Mrs. Hubbard, dusting and polishing, had seen it.

"That's a horrible thing you're making, Mrs. Leonard," she had said one day, confronting Stella, hands on hips, across the width of the kitchen table. "It isn't healthy. It makes me go peculiar. I'd put it away, that I would, as soon as you feel you are able. It's done its turn, I'd say – and it's doing you no good now. Shutting yourself up with such nastiness all morning. . ."

Stella had glared at her for a moment, outraged by such frankness, but Mrs. Hubbard had stuck to her guns.

"Miss Julia'd hate to be remembered like that, and you know she would, if you'll pardon the liberty, Mrs. Leonard." The voice was flat and expressionless, but to Stella's sensitive ear, the concern and compassion were unmistakable.

"It isn't right to make a thing like that," she had gone on doggedly. "Not to make it when you're thinking of Miss Julia."

And Stella had put the carving away, unfinished, in the dark of the cupboard underneath the stairwell. It had served its turn, as Mother Hubbard had suggested; but she had not dared to destroy it, lest the purgative effect of its creation vanished with it.

A long time ago; but the memory served to make her glad that Mrs. Hubbard had approved her eagle. She laughed again, thinking of the famous faces, the knowledgeable talents, that gathered to review her carvings. Their deliberations, their thoughtful verdicts, were not to be feared by one who worked daily under the scrutiny of Mother Hubbard. 'Not one of your best; there don't seem no heart in it.' She had heard that, once or twice, and it had always been true. How depressing if the eagle had fallen into such an unacceptable category. She only hoped that Mary . . . but it was pointless to speculate on how Mary would feel.

Her eyes fell to the letter on the desk and she picked it up a little warily. What could Mary have to say that would not wait until the evening? Or perhaps the note meant that she would not be in this evening?

The thought dismayed her; she had put off this conversation for so long, but today she was keyed up to it, uneasy with urgency, as if she was about to sit for an examination; further delay would be intolerable.

She opened the paper hastily. The note was only a few lines long. "Sorry I missed you last night," it said. "I'll see you this evening – unless you're going out. I'll be back early, anyway." So that was all right. She sat still for a moment, limp with relief, letting the hand that held the message fall to her lap. Mary was coming home. She would see her this evening. I don't know what's the matter with me, she thought. It is absurd to put such store on one day out of so many. After all, the weekend is coming. She picked up the paper again. Mary must have more to tell her, anyway; she would hardly have written just to say when she was coming home.

"My presentation is at two o'clock," she read. "And once that's over the pressure will be off a bit. It's got to be a success, Stella. It is the biggest thing I've ever handled." There was something scratched out then, but she could not decipher it, and then "Love Mary" scrawled at the bottom. That was all.

But it says a lot, thought Stella, touched and flattered. This show, or meeting, or whatever it is, she wants me to know how anxious she is about it. Despite the friction, despite the coldness of the past few weeks, she wants me to know; she wants me to share it. And to think about her.

"My presentation is at two o'clock. . ." Stella smiled, 'thinking' was the best of all the family rituals, and when the children were small, the timing of the thought had been crucial. Did Robert say he would be at the dentist at three or was it three-thirty? Was Mary's exam at eleven, or had she said they'd changed it to after luncheon? You had to get it right, or the thought might be wasted. Even Robert, flying high in his world where punctuality had no meaning, would look at his watch when it was a question of thinking – and for Mary, of course, it had been a seconds count-down. It would show unforgivable disloyalty to fail to concentrate your mind at the vital, the decisive hour.

Poor little Mary; she took things so earnestly. Even 'thinking' had brought its traumas when occasionally things went wrong, like the time that Henry had been lecturing somewhere in Germany, an important convention, a difficult, rather contentious paper. He was to give it at three o'clock. Funny how well she remembered such details. Munich, that's where he'd gone. They had put him on a plane to Munich. "Goodbye," they all had shouted, as the bony overcoat and bulging briefcase disappeared down the ramp towards the waiting aircraft. "Three o'clock! We won't forget! We'll all be thinking."

And then, at the last moment, when she had just interrupted an astonished lunch-party to explain that she and her children must have a moment or two's silence together, someone had remembered the time-change; that in Munich it would now be four o'clock; that the paper would be almost over; that despite all their assurances they had let Henry down at a time when their support was imperative. What a fuss there had been; Mary in tears, Robert in a fury. It had all been most awkward and upsetting.

143

"You could see everyone thought us very peculiar," she had said afterwards to Henry. "We will simply have to phase out this 'thinking' nonsense; it's getting out of hand."

But 'thinking' had refused to be phased out; had hung on tenaciously, surviving even the flippancy and self-mockery of adolescence, until it had become an honoured institution – part family joke, part something more serious, a declaration of involvement that united them all.

Mary's letter was more than a casual gesture. It was an olive branch, a confirmation of the bond between them. Mary had asked her, in a code she understood perfectly, to 'think', to be with her in spirit at two o'clock this afternoon. She was to encourage her through her presentation.

She must tell her that she understood – that she was alerted for two o'clock – that nothing would interfere with her concentration.

She would ring her at the office. She pulled the telephone towards her, surprised at how clumsy her fingers felt, and at the way the numbers seemed to run together, blurred by the spinning plastic disc. It made her feel dizzy again. Still it was worth a little dizziness to be able to speak to Mary.

But Mary Leonard was engaged, the extension told her politely. She had asked that any messages should be left with her secretary. Would Mrs. Leonard like to leave one now? She would see that it got passed on by lunch time. Stella frequently spoke to Mary's secretary on the phone, and she recognised the voice now, efficient and helpful. Joan? Jean? Jill? It annoyed Mary that she never could remember. But a nice, well-meaning girl; she had asked her to deliver countless messages.

This morning it was different. How could she leave a message for Mary? What could she say? 'Tell Mary that I will be thinking of her'? No. It would sound ridiculous, and Mary was sensitive to ridiculous telephone messages; she had often reproved her for leaving them, and they had none been so foolish as this. 'Tell Mary I got her letter'? But no one would telephone to make so obvious a remark. She sighed; it was no use. Anything she said would make Mary-the-businesswoman feel a clown in the eyes of her colleagues.

144

"No, thank you, er . . . Joan," she said. "I don't think I'll leave a message this morning."

"Shall I tell her you telephoned, Mrs. Leonard?" The voice was a little less friendly this time. It was Jill, not Joan. How rude of her. Why could she not remember?

"No . . . no," she said hurriedly. "It's not, it's not important. I'll see her this evening."

She put the telephone down and stared out of the window. She must not be upset. She should never have tried to contact Mary today anyway, it was obvious that she would be unusually busy.

She pulled the writing pad towards her, and then looked at it distractedly. She felt an overpowering urge, a compulsion almost, to communicate with Mary. But to write to her was ludicrous, a waste of time. She would see Mary this evening.

Yet her hands felt for the pen, and the blank sheet gaped urgently up at her. She had got to write something. How to begin? How do you write a letter to someone you are going to see in a few hours?

Indeed, now she thought about it, she realised she had hardly ever written to Mary, Henry had looked after the children's correspondence. She herself had only written postcards . . . birthday greetings . . . tags for presents. Tags for presents. She drew the pad towards her with determination. The carving was a present. It would be less embarrassing for them both if Mary were just to find it.

"For Mary," she wrote quickly, and then paused, biting the pen. What should she say? 'In memory of your Father'? No. It sounded so pompous and formal. 'In thanks for the happiness, etcetera, etcetera . . .'? Awful, those phrases; she could not bring herself to write them. This was only a present tag, it did not need to read like a funeral oration.

"For Mary – with my love." She held the paper up triumphantly, laughing at her own childishness. How could she have put so much effort into such a pathetic production? Still, it was done. She would put it with the carving, between the claws perhaps, and Mary would find it some time . . . any time. Now it was written, it did not seem to matter.

145

"For Mary – with my love." It was what she wanted to say, after all, she did not know why the words should look so trite, so inadequate. But then words, when she used them, were always inadequate. Words were not her medium. She was only fluent when she spoke through wood and stone. She had said everything she wanted when she made the eagle. It was all there, the passion and the pride and the sadness; the caring and the vision, the tenderness of a lifetime. She was giving it to Mary. If Mary could not read it, then she had failed, for she could speak no other language.

She folded the paper and sat for a moment, her eyes shut, her head hanging forward. It will be all right, she told herself. It is done now. It is finished. It's all there in the carving.

If only she could be certain, quite certain, that Mary would understand.

# 14

The stairs to the studio had grown steeper since she last saw
them – had grown steeper and multiplied, rising upwards like
Jacob's ladder, without visible end, but she had grown used to
such phenomena. She would take them slowly; would tread
evenly and cautiously. She must not grow breathless. If she had
to gasp for air she would reach the cough, where it lay inert and
torpid. She could feel it now, stirring sluggishly in the loathsome filth that had once been part of her lungs. But she must
not think of that, not now, not when she held in her hand the
message that must be put in the studio for Mary. This was a
happy errand, and it had been a happy morning. She must not
let fear or disgust cloud such a day.

She crept steadily upwards, dazzled by the sun which
poured full in her face through the landing window, and she
shielded her eyes and lifted her face towards it, eager for its
encouragement. How cold she was. Even the polished wood of
the bannister felt warm under her hand. I shall rest when I get
there, she promised herself as the last steps swam back into
focus through the myriad motes that shimmered and danced in
the sunlight. A little rest on the window seat; that's all I
need.

A rest on the window seat; there was nothing unusual in
that. She had often sat there when she had been working in the
studio, lured by the same noon sunshine, by the faded comfort
of the chintz cushions. Often she had leant her head, as she did
now, against the smooth paint of the shutters, suddenly realis-
ing how tired she was, that her neck was stiff from concentration, her arms aching from the prolonged strain of her work –
the hacking and the chipping, the sanding and the polishing.
Glad to relax here in the curious suspended atmosphere – the
neither here nor there – of a landing, where if she was discovered no one need know she was resting.

To sit in a room in the middle of the day, not reading or writing, not listening to the radio or making a telephone call, that would have been different; it would not have fitted in with the image she held of herself. But even a wiry indefatigable Stella could snatch a moment or two on a sunny window-sill without letting herself down.

How conceited I was, she thought, to be proud of a stamina that I owed to nothing but good luck. I should have been thankful, humble. But instead I regarded my healthy constitution as a virtue. I was intolerant of weakness and sickness in others. Henry's aching back, those frequent bouts of lumbago; Mary's tiresome susceptibility to colds and 'flu, the early-to-beds, the boredom of the doctor's surgery; even Mother Hubbard's endless tales of haemorrhoids and fallen arches. I hardly tried to conceal my impatience; at best I was martyred, condescending – the Stella who never had a day's illness, who rose refreshed at dawn however short the night had been, who stayed on her feet when others flagged and retired defeated. I had undeserved good fortune and I flaunted and abused it. If this horror is the price, I must pay it without resentment. Above all, I must face the children with fortitude and composure. I must not inflict them with the panic that presses upwards, that almost reaches the surface.

She eased her head from side to side. The tightness was back, like a tourniquet at the back of her skull, gripping and relaxing, the flexing of a giant hand. Pride, she thought, if everything else fails, surely that will save me? All that pride that I used to wear so inappropriately, clutching it round me like a fur coat in summer. I need it now. I need it to sustain me through the quagmire of this illness. I won't let it desert me now, when it has come into its own.

The throbbing was confusing, lulling. It seemed to interfere with her hearing. It interrupted the roar of the lunchtime traffic that rose dully from the embankment, so that it came and went in waves of sound . . . loud and soft . . . loud and soft . . . rhythmic and soothing, mingling with the tick of the grandfather clock in the hall below, with the chirp of the sparrows as they quarrelled in the tree outside the window.

She put her hands to her ears with a cautious exploratory gesture and dropped them again, relieved to find the delicate bones still intact. It was absurd, but at times like this she almost expected to find that her head had swollen in some grotesque fashion, changed as so much else had changed. From within it certainly felt enormous; she could picture it spread like a map behind her closed eyes. The area at the top was a pleasant sunlit plateau. It was here that she must attempt to remain with the everyday sounds and the reassuring present. Further down the land became wilder, at once more intriguing and more treacherous; you began to slip and slide away from reality, ensnared by memories and fantasy . . . hearing noises that were not there . . . voices and laughter . . . music playing; while far to the south lay a terrain too uncharted to contemplate, where the pulsing, gripping thing lived in darkness, over the edge of the known world. . .

Now, in the empty house, it was hard to avoid the lure of the phantom places into which she could sink so easily – where she would not be alone. Already she could hear doors opening and closing, footsteps passing, even a crash from the direction of the kitchen. And someone – was it Henry? – calling, though she could not hear the words. She had only to let go and she would be there; it was very enticing.

But it would not do. That way lay madness, senility. "And a nice thing it would be for Mary," she said aloud, touching the paper that lay crisp in her pocket, "if I were to go insane on top of everything. Footsteps and voices! I should be ashamed of such indulgence."

She sat up straighter, turning her face towards the staircase, and opened her eyes with an effort – and there before her was Robert.

He was so motionless that she could almost have mistaken him for part of the vision; but she had grown to recognise the current of energy that surged through her – and fantasy could not provoke it. It was as though she had been running on dying batteries and had suddenly been plugged in to the mains.

"It *is* Robert!" she said with glad astonishment. "It really is Robert!"

"Why so it is!" said Robert brightly, and she knew at once how foolish she must have sounded, as if she was affirming his identity to some doubtful companion.

"Fancy you recognising him!" he went on. "After all this time too! It must be fully a fortnight."

He was leaning against the bannisters, one arm behind his back, but now he sprang forward, whipping his hidden hand into view triumphantly, and thrusting into her arms a parcel wrapped elaborately in tissue paper. Flowers, spring flowers, irises, daffodils, freesias. She stared at them, mesmerised. Florist's flowers, forced and out of season, almost artificial in their lack of earthiness; yet the pang that they brought was incisive as grief, and she caught her breath sharply, turning her face away from Robert's kiss lest he read the message in her eyes.

"They're lovely," she said unsteadily. "You shouldn't have brought them. Really! At this time of year! They must have cost you a fortune."

She felt better as she spoke, the banal familiarity of the words revived her. 'They must have cost you a fortune. . .'

How like Robert to bring so extravagant an offering. He always gave lavish and unexpected presents; though, unfortunately, he could not always pay for them. When he was very small, she remembered, he just used to take things from shops and bring them to her. Later he would borrow money from Mary. The long tactful enquiries that followed had rather spoiled her delight at the time but his desire to give had always been touching, even when you suspected that the bill would remain unsettled.

"That sounds more like you," said Robert, laughing. "Thank goodness for that!" And she knew that he had caught the shadow of reproof in her tone, seen the flicker of speculation cross her face.

"I was beginning to wonder what was wrong with you," he went on. "Sitting on the landing like that. And talking to yourself, I may tell you, Mother, as if you were conducting a seance or something. What's the matter? You look exhausted . . . washed out. What have you been

150

doing? Wearing yourself out working in the studio?"

"Yes," said Stella eagerly, snatching at the excuse so opportunely provided for her.

"Yes. I'm afraid that's just what I've been doing. I have just finished a carving – you know how drained it leaves you? I seem to have less in reserve now that I'm . . . getting older. But I'm so pleased with it, Robert, I'd like you to come and see it. And it's lovely to see you, darling! I knew it was going to be a perfect day."

She got up quite steadily, clutching the flowers against her as if she were cradling a baby, and linked her free arm with his.

"A perfect day!" she repeated. "It only needed you to complete it."

She noticed that he looked startled, startled but pleased. Perhaps he had not expected so warm a reception? Was there some reason why she should not be pleased to see him? Maybe the flowers were an apology for some crime that she could not at the moment remember? She would think about it later. It did not matter now. It was enough that he was here; rather pale, it was true, and thinner than he should be – she wished that he would take better care of himself – and that now she could show him the carving.

"Come into the studio," she said, "and see what I've been doing. Then we'll go and forage in the kitchen. Mother Hubbard has gone off early; she'll be furious to have missed you."

She stood aside as he circled the bird, and laid her flowers down tenderly on the dusty table. She watched him avidly, knowing that this was one of the times that she could trust him completely. He was focused entirely on the carving, whatever was bothering him temporarily forgotten.

How lucky she was, when all was said and done, to have such a son! She could share her work with him as if he were his father. In this field he had no deceit. He was hers all the way, critical only when criticism was justified; never jealous or small-minded. It was sheer joy to watch him springing round Henry; glorious to hear him speak, in that voice that he used so seldom, stripped of its mockery, empty of all rivalry.

"It's magnificent, Mother," he said, and he came forward spontaneously and hugged her.

"I didn't think you had it in you," he went on, returning to the bird and standing before it poised, as if he had landed himself from a flight – a fledgling of the eagle that had sired him. "I didn't think you had it in you. Not any more. Not since Father died. I didn't think you would have the vigour, but I was wrong. It is magnificent. I congratulate you. You're a wonder!"

She glowed, looking up at him, and then hesitated, fingering the paper in her pocket.

"Do you think Mary will like it?" she said anxiously. "Do you think she will understand it?" She saw the astonishment in his face and went on hurriedly. "It's a present for her, you see. It's very important to me that she should understand what I'm trying to say to her, what I'm trying to give her."

Her voice petered out and she advanced resolutely and wedged the present-tag between the claws, just as she had meant to do, just as Mary should find it. This time Robert must not, as he had so often done, come between herself and Mary. It was wonderful to see him, but he must not deflect her.

She looked at him nervously, waiting for him to speak, watching the hostility grow in his face. She had known that her words might erect a barrier between them. He might not like to feel that her thoughts were with Mary, not now, not when they were united by an experience that mattered.

"And why," he said at last, "and why, may I ask, is this masterpiece to be dedicated to my sister? It seems an odd choice to me. It would be better if you were to give her an idea for a commercial advertisement."

So Robert was jealous. It was too late, she could not help it.

"It's because she needs it," she said gently. "Because she needs us, if you like. And we are here, all of us really, in the carving."

"I know," said Robert impatiently. "I know. I'm not blind; I have told you what I think of it. But what makes you think that Mary, of all people, will be moved by it? She's never shown the least interest in what either of us has striven for.

Creative effort! The thought of it bores her rigid. As far as she's concerned we are simply wasting our time."

Stella listened to him in silence, surprised at how little his words disturbed her. This was what she had feared he would say; indeed he was voicing the very thoughts that she herself had harboured, but now that she heard them spoken they seemed unconvincing. It was true, of course, that Mary might not be interested in her carvings, but she knew with complete certainty that she was interested in Robert, that in her own way she was deeply involved in everything he did. If he could not see that, perhaps she had been similarly mistaken.

"I think you are wrong," she said, pleased with the sudden strength of her conviction. "Mary is not disinterested. But she's proud and she's vulnerable. We have made her feel an outsider. When have we had the good grace to involve her? To ask her opinion? Never. But just because we haven't asked it, it does not follow that she has not got one. She would never butt in where she feels she isn't wanted. She would never interfere."

"Indeed," said Robert, acidly. "Now there, I must admit, you surprise me! I would have said that interference was one of Mary's main activities."

Stella glanced at him uneasily. She recognised that tone, and the challenge implicit in the exaggerated sarcasm. For the first time it crossed her mind that Robert might not be perfectly sober.

"I don't know what you mean," she said coldly.

"You don't?" said Robert, raising his eyebrows. Then perhaps I should enlighten you, Mother. Let's take a recent example, shall we? Of gross interference in my private affairs, for instance."

No; Robert was certainly not sober. It was often difficult to tell at first; he handled his drink with such dexterity. His body, if anything, seemed more co-ordinated; she had never seen him slur or stumble. But if I'd looked for it I'd have found it, she thought unhappily; the glint in his eyes, the edge on his voice; that intangible something, like a brittle coiled-up spring. I could have humoured him along. I need never have mentioned Mary.

He crossed to the table and leant over it, his face very close to hers.

"Well, where is she?" he said curtly. "I'd like her back, if it's all the same to you and Mary."

Stella gazed back at him aghast. Leonie and Toby. The dreadful way Robert had behaved towards them. Their injuries. Her promises. How could it all have vanished from her mind? She should have felt these emotions with all the intensity that was left in her, and instead, until this very minute, she had simply been filled with delight.

"Leonie!" she cried, before she could stop herself. "Oh Robert! How awful! I had forgotten all about her!"

Her oversight was so outrageous, her remorse so unmistakable, that the tension between them collapsed on the instant; and with it all chance she had ever had to bring home to Robert the gravity of what he had done. For she saw now that he had expected her to be angry – the flowers which lay beside her were evidence enough of that. And of course she would have been angry, very angry, if only she had remembered in time. But she had not remembered, and in forgetting she had robbed all her carefully prepared reproaches of any impact they might have carried. Under any circumstances it would have been difficult to convince Robert of her anguish and revulsion; it would be totally impossible now.

She looked miserably at the table, twisting her fingers together. At least she would not meet Robert's eye. She had brought a farcical aspect to the situation that she knew was not lost on her son. They were both well aware that she had been caught out in a failure of duty, that she felt a fool. But somehow, in the face of their own intertwined personalities, her foolishness – indeed poor Leonie's very forgettability – seemed irresistibly comic.

No. She would not laugh with him, not even though she would be mocking her own absurdity. Robert had been cruel and violent, and now she had been irresponsible and overindulgent; it was the old familiar pattern that she had vowed would never be repeated. It was not in the least funny.

He turned away after a moment, sensing that she would not

share the joke, and sat down on the step-ladder facing the eagle.

"Well, let's take the lecture as read then, shall we?" he said pleasantly. "You let me off – and I won't tell Mary I had to remind you. She wouldn't like it at all; she takes the whole thing very seriously. Although why she chose to rush to Leonie's defence like that I really fail to see. Perhaps she wanted to kidnap Toby? They say that women do get these urges sometimes."

He glanced at Stella's grim face and smiled innocently.

"No? Well, it is a bit far-fetched. But then the whole affair is beyond my comprehension. What could Mary possibly find to interest her in a vacant little thing like Leonie?"

"Stop talking nonsense," said Stella crisply.

She felt herself flushing with irritation; somewhere in her head a disturbing buzzing was beginning, but she had no time to spare for her own weakness at the moment.

"You know perfectly well why Mary brought Leonie here," she went on. "You have abused the girl horribly – broken her arm – driven her half insane by your drinking and your tantrums. Mary took pity on her, and she felt responsible for you both, heaven help her, because she loves you and you are her brother.

"It would be more to the point," she added, "if you told me what you found to interest you in a poor foolish child like Leonie. By what possible means do you justify picking her up and treating her so abominably? What horrible perversion makes you take what you don't want and then destroy it? You mystify me, Robert. You confuse and appal me."

"I can't think why," said Robert easily. "Don't be hypocritical, Mother. After all, we're so alike."

Alike? She stared at him as he sat above her on the ladder. It was hard to look at Robert dispassionately, to stand far enough away. He had always been so much a part of her. She did not see him as a separate entity, with similarities and differences that could be analysed at will. Selfish and generous by turns; introverted, yet unpredictably understanding; triumphantly fulfilling; stunningly disappointing. It was true that she had never found such contradictions particularly surprising.

155

Perhaps it was because she shared them? But she was sure she could find no joy in the misery and destruction of another person. . .

"I am not deliberately cruel," she said.

"No?" His face was insolent with assumed incredulity. "No? I can't pretend that I wholly agree with you there."

Stella tapped her foot. Robert's red herrings were always so exhausting. He never missed an opportunity to change an unpleasant subject, to deflect all criticism away from himself.

"Let's stick to the point," she said.

"But it is the point." He leant forward. The malice had left his face and he seemed to be choosing his words with care, almost as if he wished to reassure her.

"You say you can't see what I find in Leonie," he went on. "You say you're amazed and shocked at the way I behave towards her. Well, I suggest that you put yourself in my place – and Mary in Leonie's, just to complete the picture. Maybe you'd see things a little clearer then."

He's really drunk, she thought suddenly. Worse than I thought. But it did not make the words less hurtful.

"I can see no possible connection," she began, but he waved aside the interruption.

"I've watched you for years," he continued vehemently. "I've seen the way you bully her . . . intimidate her . . . crush her. Oh, nothing physical, I grant you, nothing so gross as violence. Yours is a more sophisticated kind of torture. But you've less excuse, Mother. In fact you have none. Plenty of people have lived for you. Father . . . Julia . . . Mary . . . me, if you care to count me. We have all known you through and through and still we love you. You must know that, you can't need any further proof of it. Why do you want Mab crawling on her knees?"

His eyes were on her; he seemed genuinely bewildered.

I must say something, she thought. I can't let him think these incredible things about me. But he went on at once, without giving her time to speak.

"It's different for me," he was saying. "I'm like flypaper. I attract people and then I kill them. Or at least I kill the affection

156

they start off by feeling for me. It dries up when they get to know me; they can't face what they find beneath the surface.

"Daphne. She was the last. There have been scores of others. Friends – or so I thought – as well as lovers. Even Father," he glanced accusingly at the eagle, "even Father had had enough of me, if it hadn't been for you. That's why, in the end, I came to visit him so seldom. I upset him, but for your sake he tried to conceal it. You must have known?"

He ran his hand through his hair and glared at the bird, as if willing it to believe him.

"Leonie," he went on, "Leonie happened to me by accident. She was down on her luck, but of course, you know how it was. She was pregnant by some dreary boyfriend. She told me she'd nowhere to go. She was really desperate – suicidal. I'd plenty of room and I was lonely, so I took her along to the barge.

"I never expected her to stay, and I didn't want her to, anyway, not at the beginning. But as time went on I found that nothing I did seemed to upset, even to surprise her. It wasn't as if I tried to be pleasant. I got drunk. I borrowed her money. Sometimes I completely ignored her. In the end I think I was trying to see how far I could go with her – to show her the worst in me and see what reaction it would produce. I hit her . . . insulted her . . . broke her things. No one else would have stood it. No one else ever has stood it. And I'm damned well going to keep her, Mother."

He jumped off the step-ladder and stood threateningly before her.

"So where is she?" he said. "She's not here. I looked when you were dozing and chatting to yourself on the landing. Where have you hidden her? What right have you, or Mary, to pressurise Leonie to leave me? To take her away in the night and stop her coming back?"

He leant forward so that his face was almost touching hers.

"Where is she?" he repeated. "Where is Leonie?"

He had gone very pale, but high on his cheekbones were two bright splashes of colour – the warning signs, for as long as she could remember, of a fury mounting rapidly out of control.

For over twenty years she had observed them; for over twenty years she had known what they would bring; Robert in a tantrum, squealing like a little pig, kicking on the carpet, biting the restraining hands that endeavoured to console him; Robert in a temper, slamming doors, smashing crockery, shouting at his father; Robert grown to violence, injuring a girl, threatening his mother.

She had had enough. Blessedly, cold and resolute within her, she felt her own anger rising, lifting the unbearable weight of her guilt and her love and her pity; dulling the menacing throb of the pressure that grew like a fiery bubble between her eardrums.

For a moment she feared that the words might not come as she ordered them; that the pressure might in some way cause a block. But then she heard herself speaking, quite calmly and concisely, as though the anger within her had an independent voice.

"I have no intention of telling you, Robert," the voice said clearly. "Leonie has said she wishes to leave you, and that she does not want you to follow her. She is not a dog. Although even if she were I would not return her to you if she trusted me to protect her. She is a human being with the right to make her own decision. Well, she has done so; and I have promised to respect it."

She half turned from him. The pain in her head was becoming intolerable. She did not wish him to see it in her face, and mistake it for a sign of capitulation; but he took her by the arm and wrenched her round to confront him. His hand was trembling, and there was a nerve ticking visibly in the hollow of his cheek. She fixed her eyes upon it, hypnotised. It seemed to throb in unison with the pulse of the pain in her body.

"Where is she?" he said again.

She shut her eyes.

"I'm sorry," she said. "I've explained already. I cannot tell you."

He hit her then. It was not a vicious blow – no worse than the frenzied slaps he had given her in childhood – but as his hand touched her face he let go of her arm and she knew that nothing could prevent her from falling.

She did not feel the impact as her head struck the table; only an overwhelming experience of disintegration, as if a great dam were bursting within her. It was torrential and liberating, carrying before it the anger and the sorrow, the sickness and the worry. It left her weightless, suspended in a sphere of perfect freedom, under a blinding light.

She did not know how long she lay there, floating at peace in the exquisite wholeness of her shining bubble, safe from the water that still pounded and swirled below. She would have liked to stay there for ever, but she knew that for some reason that would not be possible, and gradually she saw that the circle was complete no longer. There was a crack somewhere – a flaw in the perfection of the bright globe that held her; and through the gap she could hear a voice calling. It was faint at first, but as the fissure widened it became louder and more urgent. Someone – someone in distress – was searching for her. Someone needed her.

With an almost superhuman effort she dragged herself back from the brilliance, forced open her eyes.

Robert was there. He was on his knees; his arms were round her. And he was crying, she could see it clearly. Why should he cry when the light was so glorious, when the freedom was there for the taking?

"Mother!" he was saying. "Mother! Forgive me. . .?" His face was contorted. What was the matter. Could he not see how she loved him?

And Mary. Where was Mary? But of course! Mary was somewhere else – alone – excluded from this radiance. And she wanted them to support her. That was something she must tell Robert. Quickly. It was very important.

"We've got to think," she said.

She could not hear herself speak. How strange! Perhaps it was because Robert was crying.

"At two o'clock," she went on. "We've got to think of Mary. . ."

He was nodding. She was sure of it. But she wished he did not seem so distraught; that he would stop weeping. She tried to lift her hand, to thrust it through the thick hair to comfort

159

him, as she used to do when he was a baby. But her hand was so far away, she was not sure that she had moved it.

"We must think of Mary," she repeated. "And do cheer up, Robert. There's nothing wrong. Nothing to forgive you for. Don't be so silly, my darling . . . surely you know that nothing could ever come between us?"

There. It was said. But the magic sphere was gone and there was no refuge from the water that poured over her, blotting out the light, tearing her away from Robert. Already she could no longer see him clearly, could barely feel his arms.

Yet what enormous relief to know she could not struggle against such a deluge! There was no escape, no choice to make, no more decisions. The torrent had become irresistible . . . it was a cataract . . . an open floodgate. She gasped as the full force of it struck her and whirled her away in the dark.

# 15

Glancing round the darkened room, listening to the efficient whirring of the projector, Mary allowed herself to luxuriate in a moment's relief. It was not over yet, of course, and it was always a mistake to count your chickens, but there was no doubt that it was going excellently; that so far they were impressed.

She always mistrusted afternoon meetings, especially where Cecil was involved. They tended to start well behind schedule, and by then the members would be divided into two contingents – those who had, and those who had not been drinking at lunch. C.D. enjoyed it like that; plenty of good food and plenty of wine; a client jolly and mellowed – 'softened up', as he put it – by the effect of alcohol and conviviality. She hated it, especially when she had put a lot of work into a campaign and was pleased with what she had to offer. Like today, for instance.

But today, for once, she had got off to a good start. Basil Barratt, it turned out, did not like business lunches, did not, Mary suspected, like advertising executives very much either. C.D., condemned to a hasty sandwich in his own office, had been disappointed, though even he could see that it would have taken a car-crusher to soften up either Basil's business sense or his sales resistance. C.D. was never at ease with men whose minds worked like Basil Barratt's, men who considered business lunches to be a waste of time. With people like Basil he found that his bluster got him nowhere, and when he changed to a more obsequious approach they remained obstinately unflattered; even his third tactic, based on down-to-earth boyish sincerity, wilted pretty badly before this sort of client who responded with a blank stare of obvious disbelief.

Watching him run through his repertoire with Basil, Mary felt almost sorry for C.D. It was pathetic to see him debase himself so unsuccessfully. But there was no point in denying that, as far as this account was concerned, it put her at a distinct advantage. Today he was positively relying upon her to handle the Chairman's buttoned-up icicle of a son, who had so tiresomely insisted on coming to his presentation unlunched and stone cold sober. And I *can* get on with Basil, thought Mary, studying him covertly as he watched the screen.

His expression was extraordinarily astute, yet at the same time his eyes held an unmistakable glaze of boredom, like Stella's, she thought, when she used to hear us our homework. He's alert for any mistake, but he is longing for it to be over. Yes. I rather like Basil Barratt. I'm glad we caught him while he was doing his stint with the publicity department.

"That's the three sixty-second reels, then," she said, as the last group of films ended. "You'll remember from the schedule that we will be alternating them during the start of the campaign. The first one is an old-timer, I'm afraid, but the film people are not magicians. I thought that only one of these would be ready to show you today. They've really done wonders in the time available."

She smiled gratefully at Peter Bailie, who was sitting along the back wall behind the projector. He had brought that last reel over from the studio at lunchtime, and she was really touched at the effort they had made to get things ready. Trying to hurry up a film studio was usually an empty exercise, as fruitless as trying to open a tin with a bent tea-spoon, but she had worked with Peter for some time now, and he had gathered from her manner that this client was causing her a spot of bother. It was astonishing how kind people could be when you got yourself into a tight corner.

They were all discussing the films now. In fact, she did not like them very much, though she knew instinctively that they conveyed the impression that was needed – a new trendy approach, that did not destroy what C.D. called the quality image of the product. The whole campaign was designed to convince the public that the achievement of any ambition would be easier if you faced the world bathed and groomed with Barratts' products. You could hardly expect to be a success anywhere – at the disco, on a motor-bike, in the swimming pool, the restaurant or the golden sunset – unless you had used them. It was implicit that socially and sexually they would enhance your attraction out of all recognition. One whiff of the famous fragrance, and you would find yourself swept passionately into the nearest bed.

Old Sir Graham will have a fit, thought Mary sympathetically. But she knew he would be over-ridden. Money is money, and out-of-date salesmanship does not bring it in.

C.D. was clapping his hands, anyway; and Alan Vaughan and his assistant Terry were looking genial and enthusiastic. C.D. seemed to have done a good job on them while she was dealing with Basil. Indeed everyone had relaxed now. There was a holiday feeling in the room, as if the real work of the day was over.

They had all been very tense at the beginning, as E.N.T. had reeled out his complicated array of facts and figures; but now the newspaper coverage was approved, the posters and art-work applauded; even the convolutions of the television campaign had been explained to their satisfaction.

Usually clients were at their most difficult about the television coverage. It annoyed them that something so very expensive should be so bewildering. All those endless audience measurement figures, the discussions about regional patterns and preferences, problems about availability; and every company with a different rate card. C.D. was never a help here, either. He revelled in generalities, but was happy to leave the complicated details to humbler talents. She had struggled through pretty creditably with E.N.T. and the market research man beside her.

It was a pity that Cecil and Eddie were like oil and water. She often felt that, if she did not work for his arch-enemy, she might have grown quite fond of him. Poor harrassed E.N.T., he always looked as if he had ulcers and no wonder; it must be dreadful being a media statistician. But today he had been so kind and supportive.

I suppose everyone knows that C.D. is holding the axe over my head as far as this account goes, she thought ruefully.

Even so, it was nice to think that they had pulled out all the stops to help her, to show the client that they worked with her harmoniously. And they do, she thought warmly. They may think I am an oddity, but they do work with me harmoniously. Even Roy, whose big roughs for the posters had been shown off in his own department, had allowed her in to set up everything to her own satisfaction. He hadn't objected when he found that she had tidied up the mess in his sanctum a little. C.D. had noticed that too.

"A bit of overtime put in here, Mary?" he had whispered. "Looks a lot better for it."

She had known that was a plus – a small one, but significant. It had put him in a good mood, C.D. put a lot of store by appearances. A good cover-up was a job well done as C.D. saw it. He was the very embodiment of the whited sepulchre . . .

They were all seated at the big table now. Someone had brought in tea, though Alan and C.D. looked as if they would have liked something stronger. They were passing round a mountain of photographs, destined for the top slice of the market; for the glossy magazines.

"My God," muttered Basil beside her.

He was looking at a scantily clad lady who leered up at him from a leopard-skin rug. Newly bathed in Barratt's offerings, she was ready for anything.

"My God," he repeated. "What on earth will my father . . .?"

"He'll hate it," murmured Mary. "Mine would have, too. I've never met a nicer man, but he didn't make a penny. He wrote books that nobody bought. . ."

Basil laughed, but he looked at her strangely, as if surprised to find her here in such uncongenial surroundings.

"Well, that won't do for us," he said. "I'll have to bring pressure to bear on him. He needs a bit of pushing these days, but he'll come round to it in the end.

"I'm sure it will be very persuasive," he added, almost as if he was reassuring her. "It certainly has punch."

"Thank you," said Mary.

How glad she was that no one had brought pressure to bear

on her own father. Stella could have pushed him, she thought. He was a clever man; he'd have found success in many fields if he had looked for it – maybe even in business. Certainly Stella could have urged him into something that would have brought in a bit of money, but then Stella did not expect material rewards. She accepted that her husband's energies were happily absorbed in writing specialist books; if they did not bring in riches then she was content to do without them. It did not occur to her to question, let alone strive to change, Henry's direction in life.

It's not surprising that she does not understand what goes on in here, Mary thought, frowning at the pile of photographs before her. How could she feel any sympathy for it? But she doesn't want me to feel myself a failure. I wonder if she got my letter? I wonder if she's thinking?

She smiled. The image of Stella was very vivid. She could see her at her desk, sifting through the mail, discarding with distaste the buff envelopes, the tax demand, the bank statement, the final notice from the gas board, turning with a brightening face to what she called her proper letters, catching sight of the familiar handwriting. 'Why, here's a note from Mary.'

She pulled herself up with a start, blinking away the intrusive picture. It had been a long day, and she was tired. She must pay attention to what was going on around her. She glanced over at C.D. who was leaning back in his chair, holding up a photograph and laughing with Alan Vaughan.

Yes, it had undoubtedly been a success. In another hour, with any luck, it would all be over.

She noticed that Gay had come in and was hovering around behind C.D.'s chair waiting for a chance to interrupt him. How tiresome she was. Couldn't it keep till later? C.D. hated to have his train of thought broken. She tried to catch Gay's eye and indicate her disapproval, but she was already bending down and whispering urgently to him.

Mary watched them in growing alarm. Cecil's *bonhomie* seemed to have evaporated and he dropped the paper in his hand so that it fluttered out of reach into the middle of the table. There was an expression on his face that she had not seen before. Dismay, perhaps, or shock? It was difficult to tell, but she felt certain that for once the emotion was unfeigned. He had been taken off guard, had not had time to arrange his face. What on earth could Gay have said to upset him? Surely she could have waited until after the presentation. She must know how important. . .

But suddenly it was not important at all. C.D. had stood up, abruptly and without apology, and come round the table to where she was sitting. With distaste, she felt the grip of his pudgy hand on her shoulder.

"Mary," he said awkwardly, "just pop outside for a moment, will you, there's a good girl? Gay's just been telling me that someone's here to see you."

He propelled her to her feet as he spoke and shepherded her down the length of the table. Behind the concern, she sensed his desire to be rid of her, to hand her safely over to Gay before she had time to unsettle him further. This news, whatever it was, had clearly obliterated her value as a business asset. A moment ago she had been Mary, the Account Executive, efficient and anonymous, with no identity other than that conferred upon her by her position in Markhams. Such a Mary did not need a background; as C.D.'s right hand, even a surname seemed almost superfluous, but she could tell from Cecil's manner that the 'someone to see her' had not called in the line of business. Her visitor had turned her into a person, and as such she had become a potential embarrassment – someone with a private life so pressing that it had intruded on an important business meeting.

Good news, just occasionally, could be allowed across the barrier that divided your personal affairs from the anonymity you assumed at the office. A quick bout of congratulation when your wife produced a child, perhaps. A round of drinks to celebrate a respectable win on the pools. But bad news had no place there. You would as soon appear naked as display your worries or sorrows at a client's meeting.

It was plain then that the news was bad; that was why C.D. was hustling her from the room in evident confusion, as if she was a child who had disgraced herself at a party. That was why Gay, who had never made a pretence to like her, put her hand on her arm as she swept her through the crowded reception area; and that was why, for the first time in her life, she was being shown into what they always called the rest room – a tiny windowless tomb, reserved for people who felt ill, or had an accident, and were best concealed from view.

She hesitated on the threshold, overcome by an irrational but violent reluctance to face whatever was in there. She wanted to stay in the busy entrance hall, to remain the able successful executive who was just finishing a first-class presentation. She wanted to turn and run from the responsibility of being the real Mary, the inadequate vulnerable Mary Leonard that she had so carefully hidden from her colleagues at Markhams.

"Go on in, dear," Gay was saying gently.

Dear. Her heart sank further. Gay had never called her 'dear' before. Maybe Gay too had another personality, softer, more uncertain than the one she exhibited at the office? But her gentleness was ominous, nonetheless.

"Come along, Mary," she said again. "Your brother is waiting for you. I knew you would want to be alone with him."

Your brother. The words were electrifying, breaking through the limbo, resuscitating the real Mary beyond hope of denial.

And the real Mary bounded forward, sick with fright, and heard the door close quietly behind her.

Robert was sitting on the edge of the little cot reserved for Markhams' ailing employees, but he rose to his feet as she came in and stood helplessly in front of her. His customary grace seemed to have left him, and he moved stiffly, holding his hands out aimlessly before him. His face had lost its mobility; it was white and rigid as if it were made of wax.

Only once or twice had she seen him look like this, after that horrible car crash that had left him unscathed but had injured so many others . . . and on the barge on that flawless October morning when she had gone to tell him that Father was no longer alive. Now, as her eyes took in his dishevelled appearance, she wondered for a moment if he had had another accident? How else could he have got so absolutely filthy, his face streaked, his clothes coated in dust?

"Mab," he was saying. "Oh, Mab! I don't know how to tell you. . ."

But she knew. That dust – so fine and grey and feathery – he had been covered in it often enough during his childhood, his hair sprinkled as if with powder, his trouser knees solid and white where he had ground it in. She had seen before those same dirty circles where he had rubbed his eyes, and the long smudges where the tears had run unheeded.

There was only one place he could have been to get himself so dusty; only one thing that could have happened there to bring him to her like this, so stunned and ashen and begrimed.

"Stella!" she said. "It's Stella, isn't it? She's ill . . . she's collapsed . . . Something terrible is happening to Stella."

But she knew as she spoke that he would never have left her. He would have telephoned, asked her to come to them. He would not have arrived at the office like this, wasting time when he could have been beside his mother.

"No. It's worse than that," she said dully, and she took his cold hands and held on to them as if she was drowning.

"You've come here to tell me that Stella is dead."

# 16

The rain was confusing; its noise and persistence numbed her. It stung her face and streamed from her hair into her upturned collar. Thwarted, it drummed and battered on her mackintosh, and pounded victoriously on her uncovered head.

Sometimes she screwed up her eyes and shook her hair till the water flew around her, but it was a reflex action only. She was no longer aware of being wet, and she walked steadily like an automaton, welcoming the loss of feeling, grateful to have found a hiding place from reality in the downpour and the dark. It was possible to avoid thinking here, in this falling wall of water; possible to narrow her world to a small strip of shining pavement and the brown swirl of the gutter where a miniature river rushed briskly towards the gratings and disappeared abruptly, sucking and gurgling into the drain below.

Only Barrie, striding mute and unhappy beside her, remained obstinately substantial, looming large and glistening as streetlight succeeded streetlight, fading briefly into an enormous shadow in the blackness in between.

At least conversation was impossible, no words could be expected of her in the midst of such a tumult. The rain, vicious as a hail of arrows, separated them from each other, blurring his actual presence as it blurred the memory of the house where Stella lay still and white in her bedroom; where Mrs. Hubbard, red-eyed but solid as a pillar, kept watch over the sleeping Robert.

She felt nothing but anger as his hand grasped the sleeve of her raincoat – a wild, unreasoned resentment that he should try to penetrate her insensibility. How dare he drag her back into herself when all she wanted was to walk on like this for ever, drugged and stupified by exhaustion and the beating of the rain? But his grip was determined, and she knew with despair that her reprieve was over. There was no hope of escape anyway – there never had been. She was like a sleeper fleeing from the inexorable events of a nightmare. Stella was dead; and Robert, when he woke from the effects of his sleeping-pills, Robert would need her, whatever he had done.

She stopped and dashed the rain from her eyes. Barrie looked strained and sodden in the greenish glare of the street-lamp. She felt a longing to tell him about Robert, to share this new responsibility with him. Yet that was denied to her too; not even to Barrie must she betray what she had found out about Robert. Perhaps, if she smothered this impulse to confide in Barrie, the memory would fade? Perhaps it would be washed out in the rain, would evaporate in the turmoil of their loss and sorrow? She might forget about that hideous moment with the doctor, when she had looked into Robert's face and seen a truth that stunned her.

But already she could see it would not be like that. The scene was imprinted somewhere in her head as if it was recorded on film. It was not going to fade. She could not wipe it out. Even now it was beginning again, glaring and precise in every detail. It flashed mechanically before her, clicking over and over before her mind's eye.

There was Dr. Campbell, natty and trim, with his white spongy hands and antiseptic odour. There was Robert facing him, wild and dirty, with Stella's impossible death certificate dangling from his fingers. They stood bright before her like characters in a play, larger than life, their differences absurdly overstated. Dr. Campbell's composure was not reassuring. Exaggerated, it had become threatening. It put Robert, so clearly beside himself, at such obvious disadvantage.

Though of course that was ridiculous. Dr. Campbell had been kind. He had spoken to them gently, as if they were his own children. He had told them how Stella had been suffering from cancer, had been taking massive doses of carefully balanced drugs. He explained how determined she had been not to inflict on them the worry of her illness; how she had wanted to enjoy her relationships unchanged as long as she possibly could. Now death had overtaken her as a result of her disease and the weakening effects of the drugs essential to treat it – a cerebral haemorrhage – quick, shocking, but altogether to be expected. They must not grieve that she had left them so suddenly.

"It was as she would have wanted it," he kept saying. "She was spared everything that she most feared."

"Then she would have died anyway?" Robert had asked suddenly.

It was the inflexion of his voice, rather than his actual words, that had penetrated the fog of her misery.

"Anyway?" Dr. Campbell had said, looking up in obvious bewilderment. "Anyway? How do you mean, Robert? She had a massive cerebral haemorrhage, as I have told you."

"I meant if she hadn't fallen," said Robert eagerly. "If she hadn't fallen like that, and struck her head on the table? I . . . I was there, you see. If I had reached her, if I had prevented her from falling, it would still . . . it would still have happened?"

He sounded simple and guileless, but she had heard that tone before. Today it did not ring true; it was subtly out of key.

She glanced at him doubtfully as he stood by his mother's desk. Until now he had remained wooden and passive. 'Shock', Dr. Campbell had said professionally. 'You'd best get a bed warmed up for him, Mrs. Hubbard', but suddenly his face had come alive with the agony of his suspense, and his knuckles showed white where he grasped the back of the chair before him.

"Why, yes," Dr. Campbell said soothingly. "Falling had nothing to do with it. Indeed, it is possible that your mother was dead before her head struck the table. In any case, it was the stroke that killed her, Robert. It was the stroke that caused her fall."

Surely that ought to have reassured him? But Mary, unable to move her eyes from his face, had seen that it was not the answer he wanted. Somehow kind Dr. Campbell had misread the situation, had got it wrong. Maybe Stella had fallen first, and Robert knew it? Maybe he felt he could have helped her if he had not been so drunk – for he had been drinking, she was sure; but then Robert was not clumsy when he had been drinking, only unstable and difficult, sometimes violent.

Violent. What had he said, so innocently, just now? 'Would she have died if she hadn't fallen?' That was it. How could she have been so blind?

What did you do to her? she wanted to cry. Did you push her? Shake her? Strike her? What did you do to Stella that you think could have caused her death?

Dr. Campbell's voice had ceased and Robert lifted his head. The colour had come back into his face and his eyes were no longer dull, but the animation was unnatural. It boded no good. It was wrong. It frightened her. He looked dangerous and cruel, even a little mad.

As he opened his mouth she had known that if she let him speak she would not have to ask him what had happened between himself and Stella. He was going to tell her. And worse – much worse – he was going to tell Dr. Campbell. This was Robert out for the kill, the Robert who felt compelled to shock and destroy and wound the feelings of others; and today, crazy with guilt and grief and self-loathing, he had chosen himself as the victim.

She knew that nothing she could say would quiet him. She had never got through to him when this cloud of fury vibrated around him. But he must be stopped. It was imperative. Somehow she must, she would, stop him.

He was standing behind Stella's chair, his thin hands clenched on its back, his legs hidden behind it, invisible from the rest of the room. There was no time for second thoughts; no future in hesitation. She stepped briskly beside him and kicked him viciously on the shins.

It was a brutal kick; she was amazed at the ease and precision with which she achieved it. Never in her life had she done such a thing, nor imagined herself capable of it. She had always shrunk from physical outrage; she had no appetite for it. 'You was never a thumper,' as Mrs. Hubbard had once said, and it was perfectly true. She had left all that to her small brother.

Perhaps it had been the astonishment as much as the pain that had broken the daemon in Robert. In the seconds that followed she watched the colour drain from his face. The drink; the shock; and now the pain – he's probably going to be sick, she thought, or perhaps he'll faint. He always was a fainter. But she felt no pity or remorse, only a grim glow of satisfaction. It was as if the blow had been struck for Stella – Stella, who would not have wished her son to destroy himself before Dr. Campbell; no matter how terrible his crime against her; no matter what he had done. Even if she had broken his leg she knew she would not regret it. Anything was better than letting him go on – than letting him put into words what should, in order to preserve them both, go silently into the grave with his mother.

She had watched him sway on his feet, seen his fingers relax and lose hold of the chair that supported him.

"Thank you," he said vaguely.

In the voice, in the perfect manners, the ghost of their father flickered momentarily between them.

"Thank you," he repeated. "That was really very generous of you, Mary."

And then he had slumped forward over the chair, limp as a rag doll, the legs she had kicked sliding slowly out behind him; and the doctor had hastened forward to catch him before he slipped to the floor.

Robert lying on the carpet, Dr. Campbell bending over him. What had happened next? But she could not remember. The film, so relentless and exact, seemed to have stopped there. After that her recall became muddled and imperfect. Barrie must have come in some time; she knew he had carried Robert upstairs like a baby. And there had been tea – scalding and unwanted, but swallowed down to please Mother Hubbard, and little pills, intended for her, but handed out to Barrie as if she was not responsible enough to be trusted.

Some time, somehow, she must have found her mackintosh and escaped from their ministrations. She must have opened the door, run down the steps, started on this idiotic aimless journey that had brought them here, saturated and cold, facing each other like strangers on the deserted embankment.

Suddenly it all seemed farcical. She was acting a part, pretending to a lunacy she knew she could control. She did not need to walk in the night as if she was demented, dragging dutiful worried Barrie through the freezing rain. Nothing could excuse her for behaving so thoughtlessly towards him – not even the desolation of knowing that Stella had not, after all, put any value on her affection; had not loved her enough to think of her, or turn to her for help when she was dying.

She must put a stop to it. They must go back at once; Barrie must not be allowed to worry unnecessarily about her. He must be dried out and warmed, and made as comfortable as possible.

She looked up, determined to reassure him, and saw that he was speaking to her already.

"You're not listening to a word I'm saying," he was shouting. "I've been talking to myself, haven't I? You simply haven't heard me."

She shook her head helplessly, and he reached out an arm and pulled her against him.

"I'm sorry," she said. "I don't know what came over me, Barrie. We'll go back now. I'm all right. Honestly. I'm sorry I have made you so wet and miserable."

They clung to each other, bulky and dripping, his cold hand laced through the sodden mass of her hair. No bed, no passion had brought her so close to him; no nakedness or warmth left her so much in need of him. But Stella had not cared about her, and for Robert she was only a foil, a fall-back to be used when more important things let him down or fell from under him. Stella's death, her disinterest, had shown her to be unlovable, inconsequential; she must not impose on what was only Barrie's strength and kindness.

She broke away from him, frightened by the lure of a new dependence.

"Let's go home," she said.

The words sounded arid, empty. Where was home, anyway? Home had been synonymous with Stella, with her casual, preoccupied flash of welcome. With that extinguished, it no longer existed.

I'm being mawkish, she thought. Mawkish and sentimental.

"Home!" she repeated firmly. "We must go home now."

174

He looked hesitant and wretched. She had a suspicion he realised the effort the words had cost her.

"All those pills," she added. "I'll take them, I promise you. They'll make me sleep. You know they will."

She backed away as she spoke, but he took her hand and drew it with his own into his pocket, and they wheeled like sentries, plodding solemnly in step together, and retraced their steps through the unfriendly dark.

She stood beside her bed. The hot bath that Barrie had insisted upon had thawed and relaxed her body, but her mind was impervious to steaming water; it raced on, coiled tight, alert and far from sleep.

She looked disbelievingly at the pills that Barrie had arranged on her dressing table.

"Take them all," he had said. "They'll knock you out all right."

But it seemed impossible that anything, pills included, could quench the intensity of her wakefulness. She simply did not know where to go, what to do with herself. Never had she felt so restless, and yet so completely without purpose. She needed to see Stella. It was impossible to believe that she was not here, hidden somewhere from her in the darkened house; waiting to be wakened, waiting to be greeted, argued with, consulted.

She was not in her bedroom; of that much she was sure. No shadow of Stella attended her own body. It had been deserted, forsaken by the vibrant animated person she was looking for. Somewhere, surely, she could discover her? Somewhere there would be a trace of the elusive Stella, who so incredibly had left her without a word, without a presentiment, of farewell.

She left the room hurriedly, tiptoeing past Robert's door, flitting downstairs like a thief. The studio door was ajar, but she wavered on the threshold with her hand on the carved embrasure. She had often paused like this when Stella had been alive, afraid to interrupt her when she was working. Now she found her hesitation reassuring. It was as though there was still someone to disturb, as if the room in front of her was still occupied. She leaned her forehead against the door, nervously exploring the extent of the presence beyond it, and at last pushed it open and groped along the wall for the light.

Her hand fell from the switch as the room rushed in upon her. Beneath the unshaded bulb each detail stood out in aggressive clarity, unfamiliar and strangely hostile.

The studio had always been shabby and uncomfortable. Only Stella's current carving was ever kept clean. Dust, inches thick, settled and accumulated on every other surface, and Mary had long ago become oblivious to the dilapidation around her; she simply did not see the broken furniture and peeling walls. Filled with sunlight, filled with Stella's energy, the room was always purposeful and friendly. You sat on the backless chairs as if they were thrones, or stood by the uncurtained windows without noticing that the paint was flaking; you were always bewitched, your eyes and attention drawn and held by the magic circle that was centred upon Stella.

Now, in the night, the cold white light threw everything into prominence. For an instant Mary felt a lurch of real panic. This was not Stella's studio. This was the wrong room. It was a bad dream. An hallucination. She felt she was looking through a window at a brightly lit show-case; an ill-conceived reconstruction of something she loved, so badly done that it was barely recognisable. That pitted table, for instance; it was larger and more battered than it should be; and the tools littered over it were worn and abandoned, not at all like the ones that belonged to Stella.

The illusion was over in a moment, but it left her empty and shaken. How foolish she was to have come here looking for comfort. At best she had been barely tolerated in this room; always she had felt herself an intruder. Of course Stella's studio would reject her now. Just as Stella herself had done.

"I should have known not to come," she said aloud. "And you're not here anyway. You are not here any longer."

Her voice rang out round the empty room, bitter and accusatory. In the silence that followed she found that she was trembling with anger.

How could Stella have left her like this, uncared for and

discarded? How could she have felt so little for her? Why did this room, where some shred of consolation might have lingered, stare back at her with hostility, blank and unresponsive?

There was a sour taste in her mouth. She did not recognise this new emotion, so different from grief, or pity or sorrow. It was something she had not experienced before, born of the disappointment and the hurt inside her. Perhaps it was rage.

In any case, it strengthened her. She would not go away. She would not be ordered back to bed by the clamour of an empty room.

She looked around her coldly.

There was Stella's new carving. Someone, Mrs. Hubbard she supposed, had remembered to wrap it in its nightly dustsheet; but even the folds of dirty linen could not undermine its presence. It dominated the room like a spectre. The step-ladder had been dragged well back in front of it, and stood in an admiring posture, like a critic at a private view. At that moment she would not have been surprised if the two had begun to hold a conversation – a knowledgeable conversation that excluded her entirely. Even the chairs were pointedly turned towards the sheeted figure – away from her, as if they would prefer her not to sit on them. But I will, thought Mary spitefully. I will sit in this room all night, if that's what I want to do. Deliberately, she studied Stella's wicker rocking chair, pleased to find that the new ice forming inside her withstood the test.

As she moved, something colourful flashed at her feet, and she bent to pick it up. It was a flower, dusty and badly wilted, but still defiantly blue; still unmistakably an iris. She stood frozen, the bruised stalk slimy in her hand. She saw now that the floor was strewn with flowers, mostly lying round one end of the table. They were crumpled and trampled, as if they had been trodden underfoot in some wild commotion. That was where Stella must have stood . . . where Stella must have fallen.

She stared at them in horror. They were mangled and broken. Already they were hardly flowers at all. Yet, only this afternoon, Stella had stood here holding them, smelling them, enjoying them.

It was too much. It was as though the room had conjured up a final device with which to torture her. She fell upon the flowers in a fury, scooping them up out of the dust and thrusting them out of sight into one of the packing cases that Stella used to dispatch her carvings. Crawling out from under the table with a last daffodil clutched triumphantly in her hand, she looked up from her knees at the shrouded carving, standing detached and remote above her. It was smug. It was detestable. She felt a violent desire to unmask it, to degrade it, to prove to herself that it was less, far less, than she remembered it to be.

She threw the flower into the box and fell upon the ladder as if it was an adversary, dragging it across the floor to where the bird stood on Stella's big working block, its head just out of her reach. She had forgotten how large it was at close quarters; how ridiculously large. It was typical of Stella to kill herself in making a carving so absurdly high that you had to use a ladder to reach the top of it. Self-indulgent. Unnecessary. Exhibitionist.

She sprang up the ladder and wrestled with the dust sheet, and it resisted her gamely, catching on the bird's every projection, billowing maddeningly in her face. She whisked it free at last, screwing it furiously into a ball as she did so, and hurled it into a pile of art work that Stella had stacked neatly along the wall. The gesture was petty, but she felt heady with the lust for destruction. There was a thrill in giving in to it, even in this small way. Somehow it released the tension, the misery, the weight of responsibility.

Had Robert really quarrelled with Stella? Had he pushed her? It no longer mattered. Just now, she almost sympathised with him, anyway. Stella was heartless. She had worked here feverishly until she collapsed, creating a carving that she had not wanted to share with her. She had not even asked her to look at it. Why should she care how Stella had died? Stella had spared no thought for her. She had shut herself away selfishly with her magic and her talent. She had expended her last energies giving birth to this futile lump of stone.

It would be futile. She willed it to be futile. Somehow she felt that if she could withstand the spell of this carving, it would be easier to withstand the memory of Stella – to bear the failure of their relationship.

She took the battered rocking chair and wrenched it into position. She would sit here, straight in front of it, and study the bird. Tonight it would be revealed to her for what it was, the empty testament of a spirit empty of affection. She would not be moved by it; she would not be conquered. If she must come to terms with the fact that she had meant nothing to Stella, then at least she could make a start by freeing herself from this hurtful pretentious thing that Stella had not bothered to let her see.

# 17

The church was packed. She knew that without looking behind her. You could tell by the extent of the shuffling and whispering, by the tension in the atmosphere. People were still coming, the opening and muffled slamming of the door was interminably delaying the start of the service.

It still seemed incongruous to her that they should all come to a church to say good-bye to Stella. Stella had not held with churches, had hardly ever ventured inside one. It seemed vaguely insulting to hold a commemoration service for someone who had never found it possible to believe in a god. But she had long ago ceased to venture an opinion on what Stella would have wanted. She had been unable to gauge Stella's feelings about anything during her lifetime. Who was she to say what Stella would have wished now that she was dead? Judging by the number of people who had come to pay homage to her talent, she reflected that Mother Hubbard had probably been right anyway.

"They should get a chance to show how much they thought of her." she had said. "They'll want to thank her for the pleasure she has given them. Everyone will feel like that. Everyone who has seen her carvings."

Well, that was certainly true, if the extraordinary cross-section of people she could see from the front pew was any indication. There seemed to be hosts of artists and writers, dimly recognisable to her because of their prominence; she had met some of them on the way in and they had been distant but sympathetic, though she noticed that they seemed to be on more familiar terms with Robert. It was only to be expected that they would be there, she supposed; and the same went for all those critics and collectors and gallery owners.

She was more impressed by the miscellany of faces sandwiched among them. Ladies in furs and daunting funeral hats were squeezed against sober citizens who seemed to have rushed here from their duties. A lot of ordinary people, it seemed, had loved Stella, or been moved by what she offered them. She could even recognise the proprietor of the delicatessen shop round the corner, and one of the conductors from the No. 11 bus. She had actually seen a boy on crutches, with an unappetising punk haircut. Yes, perhaps Mother Hubbard had been right. It was probably best to allow Stella's public to pay tribute to her in the only way open to them. It was of no consequence that the whole affair was a purgatory to her; a threat to the numbness that she cherished in her heart.

She felt horribly exposed, watched by all those invisible eyes behind her, in full view of the crowded chancel to her left. She stood very straight as they rose for the start of the service, wedged between Barrie and Robert in the foremost pew of the nave. Robert looked haunted and drawn; in their father's neat dark coat he seemed pathetically childish, as though he had dressed up, as they so often had, in garments they found hanging in their parents' cupboards.

Ever since Stella's death he had been unexpectedly tender and considerate towards her. He had constantly asked her advice. What would Stella want done with her carvings? Should he sell them as there was so little money? Should he keep them? Would she want him to give them to the nation? Would she want to be buried with Father, or would she rather be cremated? And what about this service that everyone was pressing for? Would it offend her? Or would she regard it as fitting?

Why could he not see that she was the last person to advise him about his mother? She knew that it would have enraged Stella to see him deferring to her in matters where her opinion was an impertinence.

Perhaps he had never guessed how little she had meant to Stella? After all, despite the friction and the misunderstandings, she had not really known herself. Not until Stella's death. And even then, even then she had thought the lack of communion between them had been relatively trivial – a shared difficulty; something that they could not remedy, but that they both regretted. She had not realised that on Stella's part it had become a total barrier – not until she had gone to the studio and seen what Stella had made – not until she had seen the bird.

She did not know how long she had sat in the studio, that night after Stella had died. Perhaps she had even slept there on and off, hunched in the wicker chair, her arms wrapped round herself against the cold. That would explain all those jumbled memories that had forced themselves upon her, jostling each other for room, overlapping, mingling, changing. They had been frighteningly clear, and she did not believe in visions. Perhaps they had been dreams then, or at any rate half-dreams.

But Father had been neither a dream nor a vision. He had simply been there, before her, in the stone. And Stella had been with him. She had found that more shocking; more hurtful because it was so unexpected.

As soon as she saw him, she knew she had been half-prepared for Father – that glimpse she had had long ago – her own grudging acceptance of Stella's genius. Yes. Underneath the anger she had been braced, partly armoured, against finding Father. But for Stella herself, she had been unprepared. Yet there she was, within, or rather around him – an essence, an almost tangible aura of Stella – compelling, magnetic, alive.

After a while she had seen that Robert was there also; or at least some quality that owed its existence to the being of Robert. There was nothing barren, nothing stunted or unrealised in this conception of Father. For the first time she saw how necessary Robert had been in the enchanted circle that bound his parents. The patience and compassion, the completely adult wholeness of the thing before her had been made possible by the fruitfulness and humanity of their lives together; and a lot of that humanity had been born – had been forged – in the struggle of existing with all that was best and worst in Robert.

Yes. They were all there. All three of them. Everything that she had known and absorbed and loved was standing here, crystallised in the red stone of this eagle that was not an eagle; in this portrait of Father that was more than even Father himself had been.

She felt Barrie's hand now, pressing gently downwards on the arm that held the hymn-book, and she started guiltily. The singing had ended and the congregation were no longer standing. Some were on their knees; others leant forward in their seats with their faces bowed in their hands.

She sat down reluctantly. She never knew quite what to do at such moments. For her, both postures of devotion were impossibly embarrassing and hypocritical; but today it seemed rude not to try to conform. It would probably be enough for her to bend her head forward. She sat there awkwardly, trying to keep her mind blank, staring at the floor.

Unfortunately the people in the pew behind appeared to be kneelers. She could feel their nearness; their faces were almost pressed against her shoulder blades; they were breathing down her neck. She stifled the claustrophobia with an effort, clinging on to the thought that at least one of these too-close faces must belong to Mother Hubbard. Robert had insisted that she should sit in front, immediately behind them, and it was certainly a comfort to know she was there. She had been pleased too, not at all put out to find she was displacing some of Stella's formidable relations. Indeed, spurred on by the importance of her position she had surprisingly produced Her Fred, about whom they had often argued.

What a pity Stella had missed him! She had always insisted that he was hectoring and burly, while the rest of them had opted for a shrivelled gnome, cowed by Mother Hubbard's girth and personality. Well, here he was at last – a large florid man, rather bigger than the seating space available.

"*Amen!*" he bellowed behind her, in the voice of a sergeant-major on the parade ground. Stella had won another point; he was obviously determined to take on the whole congregation.

Under the pew, Robert took her hand and briefly squeezed it, and she knew at once that Stella's triumph in My Fred's fortissimo had not escaped him.

For a moment the touch, the intimacy of the shared thought, unnerved her completely. She was relying on her new bitterness, and the detachment it brought, to protect her through this whole maudlin, tear-jerking occasion. So far, it had not let

183

her down. It was insulating her from the gale of emotion blowing up from the unknown crowd behind her, and she was sure she could trust it to deafen her to the sentiment in the coming address. But loving complicity from Robert was quite another matter. Robert, especially this chastened version of Robert in Father's best overcoat, was still a potent threat to her security. She must shut him out; she would not let him lay her open to anguish. From now on, no one must gain or use such a hold over her. Hastily, she snatched away her hand.

He withdrew at once, and she knew that she had hurt his feelings. It was not difficult to rebuff Robert, despite the outrageous way he played upon people's affections. She supposed that if you came to rely so heavily on your charm, you were doubly put out when it failed. Sometimes you wounded Robert in a way you had not intended. She wondered had he felt rebuffed this morning, for instance, during that odd conversation about Stella's eagle – though she could not think what had prompted him to start it, nor what he had wanted her to say.

He had thrown the remark out casually, in the middle of breakfast, as if she would know exactly what he was talking about.

"Do you want the carving?" he had said.

He had sounded as though Stella, so prolific over so many years, had only produced one statue of which he could be speaking. Nothing except his coffee spoon, poised motionless between saucer and sugar basin, betrayed that he attached any weight to the question.

She had glanced away. On no account would she display her wounded feelings to Robert. Stella had not even spoken to her of the eagle, let alone shown it to her; any suggestion that she might keep it was preposterous. She would not have the thing at any price, to remind her eternally of such crushing indifference. Did Robert know, had he somehow guessed, how obsessed she had become with this last carving of Stella's? If that was so, at least she could not disabuse him; she could show him just how little the wretched thing meant to her.

"What do you mean?" she had said blankly. "Do I want to have which carving?"

She had turned back to him as she spoke, and found him looking at her wryly, withering her with his mother's cool disparagement.

"Oh, you know all right. . ." he had said. "Father. The eagle, if you like. Do you want to have it, or don't you?"

That look in his eye, it was so like Stella's. She resisted the impulse to do something unforgivable; to dash her coffee in his face; to hurl her refusal at him in terms that would shatter the truce between them.

"No," she said at last, hoping the pause had only underlined her detachment. "No. I don't really think I want it. You keep it, Robert. You'll appreciate it much more than I would. You know I've never been much good at understanding Stella's carvings."

Not at any price. Not even at the cost of making her look an imbecile to Robert.

He had not seemed satisfied, though, or perhaps he had only wanted to make her suffer.

"Are you sure?" he had said. "It's very good. And it's yours. You only have to say whether you want it, Mary?"

She shook her head. "Quite sure."

It was strange of him to be so unselfish about something that she knew he must covet. He did not sound particularly generous either. He sounded reluctant and resentful, as if his words were forced out against his inclination.

"Thanks for the offer," she managed to say after a silence. "It's good of you to want me to have it. But honestly, Robert, I can't think what I would do with it."

He shrugged. "Well, it's yours, you know. Just tell me if you change your mind about it."

She had wished he would not keep on saying 'it's yours' like that. It was a curiously hurtful phrase; you would almost think he had chosen it on purpose. But that did not really fit; he seemed to be deriving no pleasure out of the conversation. Indeed he had seemed relieved when she turned to other topics, and had responded to her good-naturedly, as if she had taken a weight off his mind.

The organ belched into life, and she rose obediently, thumbing through her hymn-book. It was a rollicking festive tune, not at all suitable for a commemoration service. She wished Robert had not insisted on having it, but he had been determined to choose something that Stella would have recognised.

"She never went to church except for weddings," he had said simply. "And I'm going to make them sing a hymn she knew."

So here it was, familiar and triumphantly inappropriate. And here, thanks to Robert, was Stella with it, conjured up effectively by the boisterous commonplace little tune. Stella, slight and hatless, her clothes elegantly, casually, almost insolently, thrown together – bright as a humming-bird in her embroidered cape. Today, as always, she eclipsed the rest of the congregation. They faded into the shadows of the church; amorphous, indistinct from one another. They were nothing but a background for Stella, and she floated before them confidently, brilliant and compelling in her wedding clothes.

Damn Robert. This was his fault. It was unforgivably sentimental of him to have chosen a hymn that would bring Stella among them so vividly. He had fallen silent beside her, stricken too, no doubt. But she would not look at him, she would not offer him her compassion. Why should she compound this almost unendurable memory that he had foisted upon them both?

She fixed her eyes on the Bishop. He was here, she supposed, because he was some kind of relative of Father's. Not that Father's family had ever really taken to Stella, though in the end most of them had been won over by her success, if nothing else. Their pained incomprehension had weakened before the fact that Stella had actually turned into a Famous Connection, someone whose name could be dropped into dinner-party conversation. It was difficult to resist such little splashes of vicarious glamour – not even a bishop was immune to them, it seemed.

Anyway, he would do. He was short and plain and pompous, but that did not matter; indeed it was an asset. There was nothing about his appearance that could possibly move her. She would catalogue his garments, his features, his grimaces.

By concentrating on every minute detail of his person she would force out the image of Stella. She would drown the organ and the singing.

It was an old escape route, and today she would follow it faultlessly. She would absorb herself in the perfection of her task; the finished list would be meticulous and systematic. No part of her would remain free to be harrowed by the sentiment that rose and fell and roared relentlessly around her. Nothing would exist for her outside her merciless dissection of the Bishop. She would start with his ring; its grotesque size; its colour; its probable age; its estimated weight and value; and then the repellent way it seemed to dominate him, dwarfing the pious complacent gestures of his hands.

It was still light outside the church. Below the shallow steps the street was already teeming with people. It was hard to believe that they were real; she felt so far away from them, up here, locked in her own exclusive nightmare. It was weird and lonely looking down upon them – all those scurrying figures for whom this was an ordinary rush hour, an ordinary day.

She shook the Bishop's hand and thanked him politely, wondering what he would have said if he had known how she had passed the last half-hour. The catalogue had been intricate and demanding; she had contrived to sit through his address without consciously hearing a single word. But there was nothing she could do, nowhere she could hide, in order to escape the ordeal of all this leave-taking. She would have to respond to the people who milled around her. She would have to shake their hands, accept their condolences, show them that she was grateful to them for having come. And she would not do it well. Not like Stella, beside whose poise she could have stood protected and silent.

Stella would have done it beautifully; she would have radiated helplessness and appreciation in just the right proportions. Everyone would have felt the warmth behind the sorrow, and been certain that their presence had been worth while and had comforted her. But she could not give them that reward;

whatever she said would sound unfeeling and colourless; would sound as she felt – empty and dazed and cold.

The faces came and went. Her hand felt wooden and mechanical, like an automatic arm, clasping, releasing and then clasping again.

"Thank you. Oh yes, it was terribly sudden."

"Thank you. A mercy? Oh yes, it was certainly a mercy. She was working until the end."

She smiled and nodded stiffly, racking her mind to find something relevant and sensible to say to them. It was dreadful, like holding an audience; each person demanded an intimate response that she could not give. She was cheating them, posing beside Robert as a child beloved of Stella. She was taking their concern and kindness on false pretences, as if she had been important and significant, when if only they knew. . .

"Thank you."

"Thank you. Yes, indeed. Indeed we will miss her most dreadfully."

At least it was almost over. A cold wind had got up, and it gusted round them fitfully, snatching at scarves and hats and skirts, blowing her hair untidily into her eyes. But it was thinning the crowd. She could see Robert now, still shaking hands, his collar turned up and his necktie slipping sideways. He looked rakish and wild; his good-humour seemed to be ebbing. He was going to become unpleasant soon, as he always did when his energy was spent. In a moment that alluring smile would be snuffed out like a candle; then he would be insolent, cutting. There was no knowing what he might say.

Perhaps Barrie could help. There was nothing she could say to stop him; she could hardly make a habit of kicking her brother's shins.

"Go and talk to Robert," she said nervously, giving him a little push to try and convey her urgency. "There's hardly anyone left. Get him to come away. He's . . . so tired. Try and get him to come home now."

Barrie hesitated, and then moved obediently across the steps. She turned her back on him; it would not do to prejudice his chances by staring. How would she manage without him?

How on earth would she ever manage when Barrie, like Stella before him, had lost the impulse to care?

She leaned against the arch of the doorway with her back to the deserted porch and struggled with her own mounting desolation. She almost wished that there were more hands to shake and more meaningless remarks to be thought of. Perhaps it was better to pretend you were of consequence than to face your own nothingness undisguised. She stared down the empty steps but only one figure remained, huddled up against the wind, pressed into the shelter of the parapet. The light was going and she had to screw up her eyes before she realised that it was Mother Hubbard.

She went across to her hastily, at once relieved and irritated. Of course Mother Hubbard had worshipped Stella, but somehow it was rather ghoulish of her to be hanging around in the shadows in the damp and chill of the evening. Why hadn't she gone home long ago with Her Fred? It was rather alarming how much shorter and older she looked out in the open like this, reduced by the sullen mass of the church behind her.

"You shouldn't have waited, Mother Hubbard," she said gently. "You'll catch your death of cold, and what about your rheumatics? You go into the porch and warm up a bit – I'm going to find you a taxi."

It was good to have something to do, something that would stop her thinking for a moment. She turned to run down the steps, but Mother Hubbard caught at her arm.

"I stayed because I wanted to speak to you," she said flatly. "I wanted to ask you about something."

She looked up as she spoke, and for some reason her expression softened.

"Maybe it's not the time," she went on. "You look proper done in, I can see that, Miss Mary. But I didn't get the chance earlier, and I wanted to get it off my chest. I've been that upset ever since I spoke to him. Ever since I spoke to Mr. Robert."

Mary looked at her wearily. What had Robert done now? What could he have said to shake the imperturbable calm of Mother Hubbard? Could he have lost his temper and dismissed her? Surely not? He would never be so disloyal. It was she

189

herself, since Stella's death, who had sometimes wondered if she could stand the sight of her much longer? There were so many memories to blot out, and Mother Hubbard was a link in the chain that could well be done away with.

"Well?" she said despondently. "What has Mr. Robert been saying this time? I'm sure he didn't mean to upset you."

But Mrs. Hubbard did not seem to have heard her; she was staring at her curiously, as if reassessing her worth.

"If it wasn't you, it must have been him," she said meditatively. "And it's just the sort of thing he would do. He always had to think he came first, didn't he? He never liked to see how much you meant to her. He mightn't have wanted you to know."

She glanced up suddenly, her deliberations finished. "Pardon me," she said, "but we both know Mr. Robert."

Mary put her hand to her forehead. Usually she could read Mother Hubbard's meaning easily, with the help of the few words that were offered; but today she was slipping, her instinct had failed her.

"I don't know what you mean," she said shortly. "You mustn't upset yourself like this, Mrs. Hubbard. I'm sure it can all be sorted out some other time."

Mother Hubbard was scrabbling in her bag, but she looked up as Mary finished speaking.

"It didn't seem like you," she said. "I'd have seen that earlier, if I hadn't been so upset. You wouldn't have thrown it away like that – the last thing she'd ever written."

Mary looked at her in frustration. Robert's voice still came to her intermittently, between the gusts of wind. She must take him home directly. She could have shaken Mother Hubbard.

"What's been thrown away?" she said loudly. "I'm sure it doesn't really matter."

"It was the note," said Mrs. Hubbard, suddenly belligerent. "And it matters to me – what she wanted done with her carving – even if it doesn't matter to you."

She paused, leaning forward aggressively, but Mary did not speak. Her voice seemed to have jammed a long way down, somewhere around her breast bone.

"It was *your* note," she went on more gently. "Though she often left me a line to say what wanted doing, and at first I thought it was for me. I found it – that night – when I went in to cover Mr. Leonard. Right there between his claws it was, where nobody could miss it. And I didn't move it an inch – not when I saw I'd been mistaken. I put it back again, just as she'd left it for you."

"But it wasn't there!" cried Mary. "I've had no note, no letter. Nothing. Why didn't I find it if you left it there?"

Mother Hubbard looked at her significantly.

"I don't know, I'm sure," she said. Perhaps you'd best ask Mr. Robert. All I know is that somebody had gone back to the studio. I'm sure of that, for I'd put the dustsheet on Mr. Leonard – and in the morning I found it all crumpled in a ball. And the note was inside it; I recognised the paper. Well, if that's how she feels about it, I thought, though I must admit I couldn't understand it."

The dust sheet. She had thrown away the dust sheet. She had torn it off the eagle in a fury – flung it across the room. She had tried so hard to forget that night, all the foolish hope she'd felt, her rage and her disappointment; but she supposed there could have been – there must have been – a piece of paper . . . caught in the dust sheet . . . crushed into its folds.

"It wasn't until I spoke to Mr. Robert," Mother Hubbard was saying, "that I really began to wonder. He told me, you see, that you didn't want the carving."

"It wasn't Robert," Mary said faintly. "Not this time. It was . . . an accident. He couldn't have known when he asked me. He must have thought I'd read it."

Mrs. Hubbard was lost in her bag again.

"Here it is," she said, emerging. "Here it is. I've kept it safe. And I hope you'll change your mind when you've seen it. I wouldn't like to think that Mrs. Leonard . . ."

Her voice ran on, but Mary no longer heard her. She stood motionless, deaf and blind to her surroundings, hypnotised by the paper in her hand.

Thick white paper, torn off a sketch pad; she ran her finger along the creases, holding it carefully and keeping it folded, turning it over and over in her hands. She felt oddly reluctant to open it, to end the extraordinary delirious moment. While she held it, Stella was alive again, standing urgently beside her. She was here at last, brought back by the potency of her unseen message. She would stay only for these precious transient seconds while her letter remained unread.

She no longer felt her fatigue, nor the cut of the wind, nor the oppressive bulk of the lamplit church behind her. She was back in the studio. She was standing beneath the carving. She was searching for Stella – and now she had come.

Stella had put this paper between the claws of her carving – between the claws of the eagle, where she wanted it to be found. She had been there after all, waiting with her message in the empty studio . . . knowing that Mary would come back to find her . . . that her letter would have a special significance if she discovered it there.

She opened the paper slowly, and held it up to the remnants of the light. But there was no need – the writing stood out large and flamboyant. There was only one line there anyway, sprawled out with a flourish across the width of the page.

"For Mary – with my love."

For a moment she stared at it without comprehension, pierced by the freshness of the bold familiar hand. Such ordinary words – so few, so trite, so unrevealing – but then Stella had already told her the rest. She had told her the rest, everything she wanted to hear, in the carving she had left behind her.

"For Mary – with my love."

It wasn't much – and yet she knew it was everything. It was all there was to say.